D1824384

DESTINY WITHOUT GLORY

Destiny Without Glory

*Yarn Of Destiny
Book 4*

REBEKAH NANCE

Rebekah Nance

To my readers, my dreamers, and my believers:
Never give up on your dreams.

To Grandma M. and Grandpa M.:
Thank you for all of the hugs over the years, and here's to many
more.

TRIGGER WARNINGS

This book contains subjects such as PTSD, bullying, and anxiety attacks. Reader discretion is advised.

| 1 |

Yearly Camping Trip

Calla Lilly never thought she would lose her soul to someone like Qhuvelia. But, to understand how and why Calla lost her soul to the goddess of the underworld, we have to go back many, many months to the summer before her next year at the School of the Seven Deities.

"Alright. Who's ready for our big adventure?" Alex, one of Katherine's dads asks as he, Burton, Calla Lilly, Katherine, little Celeste, Victoria, Emmalina, Ashton, Adriana, Kit and Isabella are on their way to the campsite for their yearly camping trip in one of the forests in Rosiary. They've just been dropped off by the carriages about half a mile from their usual campsite.

It's the summer before Calla Lilly's 10th year at the School of the Seven Deities. Katherine, her girlfriend and classmate, along with their friends Ashton and Adriana, are also starting her 10th year at the school. Calla's half-sister, Victoria, will be starting her 7th year, while her other half-sister, Celeste, will be starting her 6th year. The girls' cousin, Emmalina, will be starting her 3rd year.

The young ladies of Rosiary, with Katherine, Ashton, Adriana and Princess Emmalina in tow, walk ahead of the adults, chatting with one another.

"I must say that it's a bit lonely without Grandma Hazel." Celeste remarks quietly to her older sisters, cousin and friends.

"Celeste, don't bring up Grandma Hazel around Calla. You'll only upset her." Victoria tells her younger sister.

"Oh, right...sorry, Calla. I'd almost forgotten that *you* were the cause of Hazel's death."

"Celeste!" Victoria scolds her little sister.

"What? It's true!"

"While it may be true that Calla was the cause of Hazel's death, I wouldn't mind not bringing up that fact around Calla. Victoria's right, Celeste. You'll only upset her." Isabella tells her youngest daughter.

"Yes, Mum."

The children continue talking to one another as they walk the half mile to the campsite. The adults are careful to watch Calla, making sure she doesn't start any self-destructive behaviors.

Once the group makes it to the campsite, they set up their tents, sleeping bags and chairs.

"Okay. Now that everything is set up, shall we go on one of our hikes to see the view of the mountains like we usually do?" Burton, Katherine's other dad, asks.

"Oh, yes, Dad. I do enjoy our hikes together as a group." Katherine replies.

"Let's get on with the adventure!"

The group starts walking in the direction of the best view of one of the mountain ranges of Rosiary, but Katherine notices that Calla has remained behind.

"Calla? Are you coming?"

"I think I'll just wait here. I don't really want to hike today."

The group stops walking and heads back to Calla.

"Are you on your monthly cycle, Calla? I'm sure that I have some extra pads for you to use." Isabella, Calla's stepmother, asks.

"No, it's nothing like that...I just realized that today is the first anniversary of Hazel's death."

Everyone suddenly looks solemnly at Calla. The poor girl has been ridden with that guilt ever since that day.

"Calla, if I may, the exercise will help you clear your mind. Please come with us?" Kit asks his stepdaughter.

"I don't know, Dad..."

"I promise, if your mind hasn't cleared by the time we reach the view of the mountains, we'll turn right around and come back to the campsite. Does that sound fair to you?" Kit asks.

"Alright. I wouldn't want to spoil the fun for everyone else."

"That's my girl."

The group soon starts their hike to the top of the hill, which has the best view of the mountains.

Once the group reaches the top, they pause for a few moments to take in the view. The midday sun is just peeking over the mountain peak, and it's a beautiful sight.

Kit moves to stand next to Calla.

"Well, Calla. What do you think? Do you feel better now that you've hiked up here with us?"

"Actually, Dad, I do. Thank you."

"You're quite welcome." Kit wraps his arm around his step-daughter as they look at the view together.

Soon, the group heads back to the campsite, and the adults start making lunch of Hazel's summer stew, everyone pitching in to make sure the stew is as perfect as it can be without Hazel's magic touch. Well, everyone except Calla, who is looking out at the view from their campsite. Katherine walks over to her girlfriend and holds her hand.

"You okay, Calla?"

"You were there, Katie. How do you not feel as guilty as I do?"

"Well, to tell you the truth, Calla, I do feel kind of guilty about that day. I just don't show it like I should."

"So you *do* feel guilty about that day?"

"Of course I do, Calla! I was there when Hazel sacrificed herself to make sure your mum wasn't in any pain where she was."

"I know you were, Katie. I just wish I could forget about it."

"I know, Calla. But, unfortunately, you won't be able to forget about it. But maybe someday you'll be able to forgive yourself."

"Maybe...I just wish that I – that I could hug Grandma Hazel one more time."

"I know how you feel. No one gives hugs like a grandma, or even a great-grandma."

"Is this supposed to help me feel better?"

"Hey! I *am* trying, you know!"

"I know you are, Katie. Thank you."

"You're welcome. Shall we go get some lunch? It smells divine."

"I'll catch up in a bit."

After putting her hand on Calla's shoulder to bring her some comfort, Katherine walks back to the main area of the campsite to get some lunch. Kit notices his stepdaughter looking forlornly at the horizon, and he walks over to her.

"Enjoying the view?"

"Just thinking, Dad."

"I see. Is there anything I can do to help?"

"I don't believe so, Dad. Thank you."

"Alright. If you get hungry, we'll keep the stew warm for you."

Kit turns to leave his stepdaughter to sulk by herself, but Calla grabs her stepdad's arm.

"Dad?"

"Yes, Calla?"

"Does it ever get any easier? Knowing you were the cause of someone's death?"

"It will, with time, Calla. It's only been a year. Grieving isn't just a five-step process. That process takes time. And Aileen only knows how long that process would be."

"Okay. Thanks, Dad."

"You're welcome." Kit hugs his stepdaughter before heading back over to the campsite.

Once he's gone, Calla's tears flow freely down her cheeks. She doesn't want anyone seeing her like this – it would be too much for them to handle. Calla believes at times that *she* is too much to handle.

"Calla? Are you alright?" Calla hurriedly wipes the tears from her face before her stepmother can see she's been crying.

"I'm fine, Isabella."

"Calla, I know it's not really my place, but I just want you to know that none of us blame you for Hazel's death. What happened was just an accident."

"An accident that could have been prevented if I had just read the fine print...or, better yet, I had never wanted my mum back in the first place."

"Calla, I know you miss your mum and great-grandma. I do, too. But, from where I'm standing, you can either run from your mistakes or learn from them."

"My mistakes caused the death of someone everyone loved. There's no going back, there's no changing the past."

"There may be no changing the past, Miss Calla Lilly, but there is a chance at forgiving yourself, even if no one else does."

"Do you think the entire world hates me for what I did?"

"I don't believe so, Calla. Yes, Hazel's gone, but, like I said, what happened was an accident. The only thing to do now is to move forward. You can't get over a death, Calla, but you *can* move on from it. Remember how I told you about my little sister Dawn getting run over by a drunk driving a carriage?"

"Yes."

"My parents and I grieved for a long time, but, eventually, we moved on. Life doesn't stop just because someone is gone. Yes, it's extremely and incredibly hard to lose someone, but Hazel would want you to forgive yourself and move on."

"But it's only been a year since her death."

"I know, sweetie. I didn't say you have to move on *right now*. But what I am saying is that, with time, you'll be able to move on and forgive yourself."

"Are you sure, Isabella?"

"I'm *very* sure, Calla."

"Alright. I'll think about it. This won't change the glares I still get from the majority of my classmates."

"I know it won't. It's best to ignore those people, and take care of yourself by forgiving yourself and moving on. It doesn't have to happen overnight, as the grieving process takes time."

"That's what Kit said."

Isabella smiles softly at her stepdaughter before giving her shoulder a squeeze.

"Are you sure you'll be alright by yourself for a while? You know, we do worry about you."

"I know, Isabella. And I'll be okay."

"Alright, then. If you get hungry, just come on over to the camp-site, and we'll serve you up some of the summer stew."

Calla nods misty-eyed at her stepmother before Isabella walks away.

While Calla is busy looking at the view, Isabella has walked back over the group, looking back every few minutes at Calla.

"Is everything alright, Mum?" Victoria asks.

"It's just Calla, Victoria. I'm worried for her. It's been a year since we lost Hazel, and I'm afraid that we lost a part of Calla that day as well."

"Maybe if she hadn't killed Grandma Hazel, she would feel better." Little Celeste says.

"Celeste!"

"What, Mum?"

"What a thing to say, and about your own sister!"

"I didn't think that she did it on purpose!"

"You didn't think, Celeste, and that's part of your problem!" Victoria exclaims, scolding her younger sister.

"Victoria Margaret! No need to be so harsh to your little sister. She's still so young."

"Mum, she can think for herself on a lot of things, and she speaks her mind most times. Why should I be any different? You just treat her differently because she's the last child you'll ever have, so you want to hold on to her being a baby as long as possible!"

"Victoria Margaret Northrup! How could you say that to me?" Isabella says.

"It's not fair that Celeste has gotten all the attention lately. I'm still your firstborn, you know! And I always will be!"

"I know that, Victoria. And once we're home, you're grounded for the rest of the summer."

"Not that there's much left of summer."

"There may not be much left of summer holiday, but I can still ground you for the remainder of it! Is that clear, Victoria Margaret?"

"Yes, Mum."

Meanwhile, while that fuss is going on, on another part of planet Gnypso, Kazamir is busy talking with someone, and they are both plotting.

"Kazamir, I want you to do something for me."

"Yes, Qhuvelia?" Kazamir asks. Qhuvelia is the goddess of the underworld.

"I want your granddaughter's soul. *Calla's* soul."

"Any particular reason why?"

"To join my army."

"You want a fifteen-year-old to join your army? She's just a child."

"Do not tell me what to do, Kazamir! *I* make the rules here."

"I know you do, Qhuvelia. I will see if I can try to convince her to join us – to join *you*."

"Very good, Kazamir. Do not fail me. There will be dire consequences if you do."

"I am at your will and service, m'lady."

"Report to me your findings of the location of Miss Calla Lilly Morrison."

"I already know where she is. She and her friends and family are usually on a camping trip this time of the year."

"Any idea where, Kazamir?"

"In Rosiary, m'lady."

"Very good. You are to spy on her during her camping trip, and report your discoveries to me."

"What if I'm caught? I'm bound to be arrested if so, Qhuvelia."

"Make sure you don't get caught. If you do, pray to me, and I will release you from your bonds that the royal guards have placed upon you."

"Very well, m'lady. I will do as you have asked."

"Good. Leave me, and be on your way."

Kazamir bows to his true queen and boss. He leaves their meeting place and heads to Rosiary to spy on Calla from the shadows. Currently, Calla is with her friends and family, eating Hazel's summer stew.

"I must say that this stew, while it's good, is not as good as Hazel's was." Kit murmurs to Isabella, thinking back to when he first had the stew all those years ago the day he and Celeste – his late wife – met.

"I agree, Kit." Isabella remarks.

Kazamir is spying on Calla, seeing if she'll turn away from the group again to go off in the distance by herself.

She doesn't.

| 2 |

Catalina Breaks Calla's Arm

After a week of hiking, eating stew and other foods, looking at the beautiful scenery of Rosiary, and being together as a group of friends and family, Calla and the others leave the campsite to go to their respective homes to prepare for the upcoming school year. The group of students soon head to the School of the Seven Deities after saying goodbye to their own family members: Calla to Kit, her stepmother Isabella, father Emmitt, and Kit's girlfriend Inge, while Victoria and Celeste say goodbye to their parents, Emmitt and Isabella. Emmalina says goodbye to her moms, Queen Luana and Queen Consort Nona. Katherine says goodbye to her dads, Alex and Burton, and Adriana and Ashton say goodbye to their respective parents as well.

"Be good this year, and we'll see you at the end of term for the Feast of the Goddess." Kit tells his stepdaughter.

"I will, Dad. See you soon."

"Call me if you need anything, and Grandma, Grandpa and Aunt Kessia, as well as your Great-Aunt Rose and Great-Uncle Edison and cousins Harris and Giana, are just a phone call away. Don't hesitate to call them if an emergency arises, Calla."

"I won't, Dad."

"That's my girl. Have a good term. And look after each other!" Kit adds as his stepdaughter embarks the carriage with her sisters and cousin.

"We will, Dad!" Calla calls out to her stepfather.

The seven students of the School of the Seven Deities soon reach the school in Eburnean, and they leave the carriage after their bags are taken off and out of the carriage.

"Welcome, students, to your next year at the School of the Seven Deities." Headmistress Ella-Rose West says, stepping up to the arriving students.

"Calla, my dear! So lovely to see you again! Your Auncle Asmi has missed seeing you over the summer." Asmi says, wrapping their arms around their favorite niece.

"Auncle Asmi, you're squishing me."

"Oh, I'm sorry, Calla."

"Thank you."

"You're welcome." Asmi says as they and Calla walk toward the school together.

"Now, Calla, if any of the other students pick on you for Hazel, come see me as soon as possible so we can work through your guilt and whatnot."

"Yes, Auncle Asmi."

"That's a good girl. Now, run along and get ready for dinner."

"Yes, Auncle Asmi."

Calla walks with her classmates and family members to the dining hall, where dinner will begin in just fifteen minutes. As is protocol, the students must stay silent and still as they're being served their dinner, until everyone has been served, and then the students and faculty may chat amongst themselves.

Catalina scowls as she sees Calla sit down; the two have been rivals since Calla's first day at the school two years ago. Catalina is on probation for poisoning Queen Luana.

"Well, well, well. If it isn't Miss Calla Lilly Morrison! Come to grace us with her presence once again."

"Leave me alone, Catalina. I've had a long and hard summer."

"Aww...you poor, poor thing. But no one has had a summer harder than me, Calla. I had to do community service *all summer long* because of my poisoning the queen."

"Maybe if you hadn't poisoned the queen, you wouldn't have had as hard a summer."

"Maybe if Hazel were still here, you wouldn't feel so guilty about murdering her."

"I didn't –" Calla says rather loudly before lowering her voice.

"It was an accident, Catalina."

"Accident, shmaccident. What matters now is that Hazel is dead, because of you."

"I can't change the past, Catalina. My stepmum said that – "

"Whatever your stepmum said doesn't matter. What matters is that I am going to make your life a living hell this year."

"What makes you say that?"

"Because I don't *like* you, Calla Lilly Morrison. I never have and I never will. We're rivals for a reason."

"And what exactly is that reason?"

"Because I hate you!" Calla Lilly gasps as she sits back in her seat.

"I'm done talking to you, Catalina. Now leave me alone."

Catalina scoffs before turning away from Calla to eat her food.

Katherine turns to her girlfriend.

"What was *that* all about, Calla?"

"She hates me."

"Who hates you?"

"Catalina. She told me herself."

"Well, don't listen to her, Calla! She's only going to irritate you more than need be."

"I understand, Katie. I won't listen to her anymore."

After dinner has finished, each gender heads to their own dormitories for the night.

The next day, after one of Calla's last classes for the day, she's walking around the school, trying to clear her head before heading to the dormitories to work on some of her homework before dinner.

"Well, well, well, if it isn't Calla Lilly."

"What do you want, Catalina?"

"What I told you last night: to make your life a living hell."

"Leave me be, Catalina."

"No." Catalina suddenly shoves Calla out the back door down the stairs onto the soccer/lacrosse field, where it's raining and the ground is covered in mud, throwing her books, papers, binders and school supplies everywhere.

"Don't move a muscle, Miss Calla. It'll only make me want to hurt you more." Catalina leaves, chuckling to herself.

As soon as Calla is sure Catalina is gone, Calla tries to get up by bracing herself on her left hand, but she cries out as searing pain shoots up her arm.

"Oooh, oh, dear. I think I broke my left arm."

"Calla? Is that you?" Katherine can barely see her girlfriend through the pouring rain.

"Katie? I'm down here!"

"Whatever are you doing out in the rain? And why are your books and things scattered around you?"

"It was Catalina. She told me last night she'd make my life a living hell this year. I guess she's keeping her promise."

"Oh, you poor thing! Let me help you up."

"Careful, Katie. I think I broke my left arm."

"You mean, you think *she* broke your left arm."

"That, too."

Katherine, getting covered in mud and rain, helps Calla gather her things and put them in her rain-soaked backpack before taking her to the nurse's office.

"Girls! Why are you both so covered in mud?" Nurse Morgan inquires.

"It was – it was Catalina, ma'am."

"Catalina? Catalina West?"

"Yes, ma'am. She pushed me down the back stairs and I think she broke my left arm."

"Oh, you poor dear. Come behind the curtain, and I'll fix you right up."

"Thank you, Nurse Morgan."

"You're quite welcome, dear. Katherine, be a gem and go let Headmistress West know of this latest development, will you?"

"Right away, ma'am. Feel better soon, Calla!"

"I hope to, Katie!"

Katherine walks from the nurse's office to the headmistress' office and finds Headmistress West on the phone. Headmistress West notices Katherine and puts her pointer finger up as if to say "just a moment".

Soon, the phone call has ended, and Headmistress West beckons Katherine forward.

"Katherine Griffiths, do you wish to tell me why you're covered in mud?"

"Yes, ma'am. You see, I was walking back from my last class when I noticed the back door to the soccer and lacrosse field was open. Calla called out to me, and she told me she think Catalina broke her left arm."

"And where is Calla now?"

"She's with Nurse Morgan, ma'am."

"Very good. I'll call Catalina in here later once Calla is all patched up so we can get things straight. I'll have to call Calla's stepfather, of course."

"Yes, ma'am. Would you like me to relay this information to Calla?"

"That would be fine, Katherine. Off you go."

Katherine leaves the headmistress' office, still covered in mud, and heads back to the nurse's office.

"Calla? I talked with Headmistress West, and she's going to call you and Catalina in later to sort things out. Headmistress West will also call your stepfather."

"Thank you, Katie, for telling me this."

"How's your arm?"

"Still hurts. Nurse Morgan took an X-ray, and it's definitely broken."

"And that's your dominant arm, right?"

"Yes, it is, Katie."

"We'll see what the headmistress says once you're ready to go see her about what happened between you and Catalina."

"I'm just about finished up here, Miss Katie. I just need to clean her up a bit, get rid of the mud on her. It's everywhere. It shouldn't take too long."

"I'll wait out here."

"Alright. We'll be just a few minutes."

A few minutes pass, and Calla emerges from behind the curtain, hair and skin cleaned up and dried, and wearing a new – and clean – uniform. Her left arm is in a sling.

"Alright, Miss Calla. You and Katie head to the headmistress' office, and I'll see you in a week to check the progress of your arm's healing."

"Okay. Thank you, Nurse Morgan."

"You're welcome. Off you go."

The two young ladies head to Headmistress West's office, where her door is open.

"Come in, ladies. Catalina has yet to arrive."

"I'm here, Mum!"

Calla and Katherine turn around to see Catalina running up the stairs to her mother's office. Catalina sputters once she sees Calla.

"Calla Lilly? What are *you* doing here?"

"Come in, you three. We have a lot to discuss."

Catalina scowls as Calla and Katherine pass her before going into the office herself.

"What's that abomination doing here?" Catalina asks, noticing Asmi standing next to Headmistress West.

"Well, I never!" Asmi mutters to themselves.

"Catalina! Asmi is *not* an abomination. They are the school counselor."

"Oh, whatever. Why was I called in from soccer practice?"

"Because you broke Calla Lilly's arm!"

"I did no such thing, Mum!"

"Katherine told me everything, Catalina Julie, and Katherine is a terrible liar. No offense, Katherine."

"None taken, Headmistress West."

"Now, then. We must discuss your punishment, Catalina. Calla, you may tell your side of the story first. Catalina, not a peep out of you!"

"Yes, Mum." Catalina says, looking downcast.

"Calla?"

"Yes, ma'am. It all started after my last class of the day."

As Calla tells her side of the story of how Catalina broke her arm, Kazamir has just left school grounds, having been told by Qhuvelia to go into Catalina's mind and force her to push Calla down the back stairs into the soccer/lacrosse field.

Kazamir meets Qhuvelia in a forest of Eburnean.

"Well, Kazamir? Is it done?"

"Phase one of the plan is complete, m'lady. I had Catalina push Calla Lilly down the stairs, and Calla's dominant arm was broken. She's left-handed because of me, you know."

"Yes, I know." Qhuvelia sneers.

"What is phase two of the plan, m'lady?"

"Phase two is to make Calla regret Hazel's death...and I know just how to do it."

While Qhuvelia drones on about how to make Calla regret Hazel's death even more than she already does, Kazamir is thinking about how he had forced Catalina to poison Luana.

If Hazel hadn't been there to give Luana the antidote, Catalina would probably have been put to death for poisoning the queen, and Kazamir doesn't want that to happen, for Catalina is the vessel to hurting Calla.

Meanwhile, back with Calla, Catalina, Katherine and Headmistress West, Calla has just finished telling her side of the story.

"Catalina West, I am very disappointed in you, and I hereby sentence you to detention until Calla's arm has completely healed, and you are not allowed to interact with Calla or Katherine until then. Is that clear?"

Catalina moves to speak her mind, but a stern look from her mother makes Catalina purse her lips.

"Yes, Mum."

"Calla, I wish you well while your arm is healing from this terrible incident."

"Thank you, Headmistress West."

"You're welcome. Katherine, I suggest you take notes and tests for Calla while her arm is healing. Do you have any objections to this?"

"No, ma'am, but what about my own assignments and tests?"

"I will let the faculty know to give you a reprieve for the time being."

"Thank you, ma'am."

"You're welcome. You three are dismissed."

The three girls head out of the headmistress' office and Catalina sulks ahead to the dormitories while Calla and Katherine hang back a ways to let Catalina go in front of them. Catalina will serve detention after dinner.

Once Calla and Katherine make it back to the dormitories, Katherine helps Calla do her homework for the night before the two head down to dinner. They sit a ways away from Catalina and her friends so they are not disturbed by Catalina.

"Would you like me to feed you, Calla, or can you handle it on your own?"

"I'm sure I can handle it, Katie, but thank you."

Calla and her classmates eat their food and chat with one another before heading back to their own dormitories, which are separated by year and gender.

Once the students head back to their assigned dormitories, they settle in for the night after Katherine and Calla sit together to video call Kit.

"Is that my favorite stepdaughter?"

"Da-ad, I'm your only stepdaughter."

"I know, I know. Headmistress West called me and told me about your arm. Are you in much pain?"

"No, Dad. Not really. Also, Katherine's here, in case you hadn't already noticed."

"Hello, sir." Katherine greets Calla's stepdad.

"Hello, Katherine. How have you been?"

"Fine, sir. I've been just fine. Headmistress West said that I could have a reprieve from my assignments and tests while Calla's arm heals so I can take notes and tests for her."

"You're a good friend, Katherine, and I'm sure you're also a great girlfriend."

"Thank you, sir. That means a lot to me that you'd say that."

"You're welcome. Now, Calla, don't put pressure on your girlfriend to do your homework and tests for you. *You* have to supply the answers."

"I know, Dad."

"And I won't let her, sir. I know she'll have to supply the answers, but there's a plus side to this ordeal."

"Oh?" Calla and Kit ask at once.

"I'll be learning along with Calla. She and I have the same classes, just at different times during the day, so I'll be able to learn alongside her."

"Quite smart thinking, Katherine."

"Thank you, sir."

"You're welcome. How are your fathers doing?"

"Alex and Burton? Oh, they're doing quite well, sir. Thinking of getting a dog, so I'm pretty excited." Calla lights up at this, and Kit notices.

"No, Calla, I'm not getting you a dog. Not until you've graduated. A dog is a lot of responsibility, and I'd expect you to help take care of them: feeding them, walking them, bathing them, taking them to the vet...it's a lot to deal with."

"I know, Dad. I've seen movies of people having dogs."

"I know you have, Calla. If you get good grades these next three years of school, I'll *think* about getting you a dog."

"You will?!"

"I said I'd think about it, Calla. Nothing more, nothing less."

"I guess I can live with that, Dad."

"Good."

"Speaking of dads, I'd better call my own fathers before Calla and I head to bed. I'll talk to you soon, Kit. Calla, I'll see you in the bedroom, okay? You let me know if you need help getting ready for bed or anything, alright?"

"Thanks, Katie. You're a gem." Calla tells her girlfriend.

"My pleasure, darling." Katherine kisses Calla on the side of her head, and both girls blush as they remember Kit is watching them.

"Good night, sir."

"Good night, Katherine."

As soon as Katherine is out of eyesight and earshot, Calla is looking after her girlfriend wistfully.

"What's that look for, Calla?"

"Huh? Oh, nothing, Dad. Do you remember how I thought I was aromantic until I met Jenna, Carceia's daughter?"

"I do."

"I have nothing against aromantic people, but Katie and I have been talking, and we think we're both asexual. This is kind of too much information for me to talk about with my stepdad, but...Katie and I, we haven't had sex yet, but not because we're not ready...we just don't experience sexual attraction with each other."

"Oh, really?"

"I talked to Katie during dinner about telling you. I just...don't want you to be ashamed of me."

"Ashamed of you? Calla, I'm surprised."

"You are?"

"Yes. I could never be ashamed of you. Blood related or not, you're my daughter, and nothing can or will ever change that."

"You really mean that, Dad?"

"I do mean that, Calla."

"Thank you, Dad."

"You're welcome. Now, tell me, when did you and Katie find out that you think you're asexual? Did you find out together or separately?"

"Well, to tell you the truth, Dad, Katie and I found out at separate times. I was just thinking that I don't experience sexual attraction, and I told Katie and she said she doesn't either, so we came out to each other as asexual lesbians. And, yes, Dad, she knows that I'm telling you that we're both asexual lesbians. And her fathers do know. But no one else knows. They know we're a couple, but they don't know we're asexual. Do you get what I mean?"

"I do, Calla, and I'm so proud you've figured yourself out. But, like I've told you before in the past, coming out is a process, and a process that never ends. You have to keep coming out to all sorts of different people."

"Thank you for the advice, Dad. It truly means a lot to me."

"Relay this information to Katherine, will you?"

"Sure, Dad."

"So...anything you'd like to tell me?"

"Well, the beginning-of-the-school-year feast is coming up, and it's – it's on what would have been Grandma Hazel's next birthday."

"Oh, really?"

"Yeah. And I'm afraid that people will give me harsh looks or say harsh words to me in regards to Grandma Hazel's death. Don't people know I couldn't feel more guilty?"

"I'm sure they do, but people can be relentless with their teasing, Calla. If the teasing doesn't let up, let Headmistress West know, or talk to your Auncle Asmi about your troubles."

"I guess I could do that. Thanks for the advice, Dad."

"You're welcome. Love you, kiddo."

"Love you, too, Dad. I'd better head to bed. It's getting late."

"That it is, Calla. That it is. Good night, Calla."

"Good night, Dad."

While Calla has been talking to her stepdad, Catalina has been spying on her and eavesdropping on her conversation with Kit. She plans to use Calla and Katherine's new discovery about themselves to her advantage.

"This will destroy Calla Lilly Morrison once and for all."

Meanwhile, Kazamir is out talking to Qhuvelia, who is praising him on a job well done of getting Catalina to push Calla down the stairs.

"She's getting more tired of Catalina's antics, and we must use that to our advantage, Kazamir. See what else you can find out about her...anything that would be useful to me."

"Right away, m'lady." Kazamir says.

"And make sure you actually succeed this time, Kazamir. I don't want what happened with Luana to happen to Calla. That is, I don't want anyone to be around when Calla's downfall begins."

"I am at your service, m'lady."

| 3 |

The Beginning-of-the-School-Year Feast

The day after Kit, Calla and Katherine conversed, preparations for the beginning-of-the-school-year feast for the following evening begin, with the 10th years in the kitchen making all sorts of dishes.

The 10th years plan on making Hazel's summer stew as the main course, but there's tension in the air, for Hazel wasn't just loved deeply, but she was also loved widely, and Calla's mistake has affected all the students, with everyone knowing that her mistake cost Hazel her life.

While in the kitchen, Catalina prompts her classmates to give harsh looks to Calla, which isn't hard for them to do. Soon, the looks become overwhelming for Calla, and she rushes out of the kitchen in tears. Her girlfriend, Katherine, follows her to the bathroom. Calla has locked herself in a stall, Katherine not making it to be in the stall with her. Katherine knocks on the door.

"Calla? Don't pay those bullies any attention! They don't know how guilty you feel."

"But they do, Katie. My stepdad said so."

"No offense, but your stepdad probably doesn't know what it's like to be in your position."

"That's true. Oh, what should I do, Katie? Ignore the bullies? Talk to Headmistress West? Talk to my Auncle Asmi?"

"I – I don't know, Calla."

"Is there anything you *do* know, Katie?"

Katherine is hurt by this.

"I'm just trying to help, Calla!"

"I know you are, Katie, and I'm sorry."

"It's alright. I'm sure you're under a lot of pressure, with trying to perfect Hazel's stew."

"But I don't have the magic touch she did."

"I know you don't, Calla. But you have magic! That's something a lot of people here don't have, so you should consider yourself lucky."

"Lucky? I feel like the unluckiest person in the history of Planet Gnypso."

"I'm sure you do, Calla. Why don't we go talk to your Auncle Asmi? I'm sure they'd be able to help you!"

"I don't know..."

"Is there anything you *do* know, Calla?"

"Very funny."

"I'm serious, Calla."

"I don't know! I don't know what I don't know! All I know is that my life has turned to crap ever since Grandma Hazel died!"

"I'm sure you feel alone, Calla, but trust me when I say that you are not alone. You're never alone, Calla. You've got me, and you've got your friends and your family members. Come with me to talk to Asmi. I know they'll be able to help you."

"If you're sure, Katie."

"Have I ever steered you wrong, especially when your mental health is at stake?"

"How do you know my mental health is at stake?"

"Because I've been where you are, Calla. I know what it's like to feel this low. Catalina and I – we didn't used to be rivals or enemies. We actually used to be friends – *best* friends."

"So, what happened?"

"She got jealous when you came along. She thought I was replacing her with you."

"Wait a second, she was jealous of – of me?"

"Yes. And she has every right to be jealous."

"She does?"

"Yeah, because you're such a better friend than she was."

"You really mean that, Katie?"

"I do. Will you come out now?"

Calla opens the stall door just a crack.

"I guess I can't stay in here forever, can I?"

"No, you can't. Come on, let's go see Asmi."

"A-alright."

Once Calla and Katherine exit the bathroom, Catalina is waiting for them.

"Awww, were you two homos making out after Calla stopped crying? How sweet."

"Leave us alone, Catalina. We know *you're* the one who prompted our classmates to give Calla harsh looks."

"I have no idea what you're talking about."

"Don't play dumb with us."

"I'm not playing dumb or anything else. I really don't know what you're talking about. I was on my way into the bathroom to freshen up when I heard Calla crying. So, I waited out here for you two to come out – pardon the pun there."

"Look, Catalina. Leave Calla alone, and, for that matter, leave me alone as well!"

"Why should I? Everyone knows that you replaced me with this royal freak!"

"She's not a freak, Catalina!"

"Oh, please. Everyone knows she's the only royal spell caster here."

"What does that matter?" Calla asks.

"It matters because I'm going to make *both* of your lives a living hell, until you surrender to Qhuvelia."

"Who's Qhuvelia?"

Catalina blinks and shakes her head.

"I have no idea who you're talking about."

"But you just said – "

"Out of my way, freaks." Catalina pushes past Calla and Katherine, who are both looking very confused.

"Come on, Calla. Let's go see Asmi."

"Catalina's acting strange, isn't she?"

"No stranger than usual, Calla."

Calla and Katherine head to the counselor's office and Katherine knocks on the door.

"Come in."

Katherine and Calla walk into the office, hand-in-hand.

"Well, aren't you two a pretty sight?"

"Auncle Asmi...Calla needs to talk with you."

"I'm all ears, Calla. What seems to be the problem?"

"Well, Auncle Asmi, the problem is that Catalina keeps bullying me, and she prompted everyone to give me harsh looks because of what happened with Hazel."

"Burn her at the stake!"

Katherine and Calla both look shocked.

"Sorry. Old habit of mine. You were saying, Calla?"

"I was just saying that Catalina keeps bullying me...how do I put her in her place and get her to stop picking on me?"

"The thing to do, Calla, is to turn the other cheek, and be honest with her. Tell her how much you've been hurt by her."

"Is that all I can do? I want to crush her like a bug, Auncle Asmi!"

"That wouldn't be wise, Calla. Then *you* would be seen as the bully, and no one here wants it to turn out that way for you."

"Alright, Auncle. I'll try to turn the other cheek and be honest with Catalina."

"Good."

There's suddenly a scream from the courtyard.

"Stay here, girls. Auncle Asmi is on the case!"

Despite what Asmi said, Calla and Katherine follow them to the courtyard at a distance. Once they reach the courtyard, Calla and Katherine see what had caused the screaming: a group of orcs have made their way onto the school grounds.

"Stay back, you two. I don't want either of you getting hurt."

"But I can help, Auncle Asmi! Gather all the spell casters you can find, and bring them to me! I have a plan."

"No, Calla. If your stepfather knew what you were about to do, he'd have your head *and* mine."

"But Auncle Asmi! Please, you have to listen to me! I know what to do! Who do you think brought Kazamir to justice last year? Who defeated him in a magic duel?"

Asmi sighs.

"Very well," they say, "but you better not get yourself hurt."

"I won't, Auncle."

"Good. Katherine, you're with me so I can protect you. I'll send the other spell casters to you, Calla. And try not to make a mess of things and keep yourself intact."

"Yes, Auncle."

Soon, the students and faculty that are spell casters are shown the way to where Calla is waiting for them so she can tell them her plan.

"Alright." Calla whispers, "My plan is for us to collectively use 'Lightning Basalt', and that will hopefully kill the orcs."

"Good plan, Calla."

"Thank you, Guinevere. We must all say it at once."

The group of spell casters, young and old, all gather together in front of the assembly of orcs. Each member of the group, minus Calla, takes out their ball of magic yarn and they all whisper "Lightning Basalt" together.

"You really think a bit o' string will defeat us?" The leader of the orcs starts to laugh before the lightning strikes him dead, along with his companions.

The orcs all fall to the ground, dead.

"Three cheers for Calla Lilly Morrison, who has helped to save us all! Hip, hip!"

"Hooray!"

As the students and faculty all cheer for Calla and the other spell casters, Catalina makes her way beyond the school grounds, and she comes across Kazamir.

"Who are you, and what are you doing here?"

"What I'm doing here is of no concern to you, little one."

"I'm not *that* little! I'm 15!"

"That is of no concern to me. But what *is* of concern to me is the fact that I want to help you make Calla Lilly Morrison's life a living hell."

Catalina hesitates before speaking.

"How so?"

"I will give you some tasks to perform to make Calla's life so miserable, she will want to sell her soul to make sure that she never feels that low again."

"Like what?"

"Well, you've already broken her arm and made her cry..."

"I did?"

"Yes, my child, *you* did those things. It was not I who did those horrible things to her. My point is that I need you to be my vessel of power. Through you, I will be able to crush Calla Lilly's spirit once and for all."

"What's in it for me?"

"Clever girl. What could be in it for you? Is there anything you want?"

"I – I want my best friend Katherine Griffiths back."

"Well, with Calla Lilly soon to be out of the picture, Katherine Griffiths will have no choice but to return to you as your best friend. Have we got a deal?"

"What exactly do I have to *do* to Calla?"

"You must follow my directions precisely. Once you get rid of Calla's being Katherine's girlfriend and best friend, you'll be able to be Katherine's best friend once again. Now, you must publicly out them as asexual."

"How did you know about them being asexual?"

"I have eyes and ears everywhere, Miss Catalina. But that is of no concern to you. What *is* of concern to you is that you will announce their asexuality publicly at the front of the dining hall."

"Are you sure *that's* what you want me to do to crush Calla Lilly's spirit?"

"Absolutely, Catalina. You do this, and I will make sure you're in Her Wickedness' good graces."

"*Who's* good graces?"

"*Qhuvelia's* good graces, my child. If you do this, you will surely be able to have the chance to reign at her side."

"And who is Qhuvelia?"

"Why, she's the goddess of the underworld, of course."

"The – the goddess of the underworld?"

"Yes."

"I don't know...I don't know if I want to *be* in her good graces."

"You must, Catalina! You must do this for me! Because if you don't, I'll – I'll – "

Catalina backs up in fear, which causes Kazamir to soften his tone.

"I'll surely get into trouble with the law again. And you wouldn't want that to happen to your old grandpappy, now would you?"

"N-No. Wait, did you say - ?"

"Yes. I'm your grandfather, Catalina. You and Calla are not just rivals, but you're also cousins."

"Cousins?!"

"Yes. You and she have the same grandfather, just different grandmothers. So you are *technically* half-cousins, but still cousins nonetheless."

"I never knew...I never thought I had any cousins. Wait, does that make me a royal as well?"

"No, of course not! You have a different mother than Calla had."

"Oh." Catalina, of course, is a bit disappointed that she's not a royal.

"Do we have a deal, Catalina?"

"Yes, grandfather."

"Good. And considering your soul belongs to Qhuvelia already, I can already see you're in her good graces."

While Calla and the other spell casters are still being celebrated by almost everyone at the School of the Seven Deities, Catalina is on her way to her mother's office. Not because she's in any trouble, but because she wants to interrogate Headmistress West about her grandmother's love life.

Catalina quite literally barges into the headmistress' office, just as her mother is finishing up a phone call.

"Catalina! Whatever are you doing interrupting me? I was in the middle of some very important work."

"I'm sorry, Mum, but this is important. Calla and I – we're not just classmates, we're also half-cousins."

"And how did you come to know about this information?"

"Well, I – I met my grandfather."

"That's impossible. Your grandfather died before I was born."

"No, he didn't! Kazamir – his eyes are like Hazel's. I'd know them anywhere."

Headmistress West takes off her glasses and walks around the desk.

"Catalina, tell me. Did you hit your head? Well, did you?"

"No, Mum! I know what I saw! I can show you exactly who I met! He's been controlling me somehow – making me hurt Calla."

"I find that very hard to believe, Catalina. How can someone *make* you hurt someone else?"

"All I've wanted to do is *befriend* Calla. Yes, I *was* jealous of her at first and I did punch her in her nose, but that was almost two years ago. I've matured, Mum."

"You mean to tell me someone is forcing you to do these things to poor Calla? And you didn't think to tell me?"

"No, Mum. The thing is – Kazamir – that is, my grandfather – told me my soul has been sold to Qhuvelia."

Headmistress West grips her desk, knuckles going white.

"Are you sure?"

"Yes, Mum. I wouldn't lie about this."

"How do you know you sold your soul to the goddess of the underworld?"

"Because Kazamir has been controlling me – looking through my eyes, I guess, and making me do horrible things to Calla."

"So – you've been possessed by someone or something? I must find someone that can extract this entity from you so your soul can be pure and ready for the Broken Realm."

"Mum! Kazamir told me I'd be able to reign by Qhuvelia's side!"

"You will do no such thing, Catalina! You're still just a child! And I'll not have my only daughter be possessed by some – some demon!"

"Mum! Why didn't you tell me about my grandfather?"

"Because, Catalina, I didn't even know he was my father! I thought my father had died before I was born! At least, that's what your grandmother has told me throughout my life."

"You thought wrong, Mum."

Catalina storms out of her mother's office and heads to the dining hall, where everyone is eating dinner.

"Everyone! May I have your attention, please? I have an important announcement to make to all of you!"

No one can hear Catalina over the din of the students talking with one another.

Catalina takes an empty pot from one of the cooks and bangs it, making everyone in the hall turn their heads and look at Catalina.

"I have an announcement to make about Calla Lilly Morrison and Katherine Griffiths. Not only are those two girls in love and infatuated with one another, but they are also asexual."

People begin to murmur, turning their heads to see Calla and Katherine.

"Well, what are you doing just murmuring? Jeer at them!"

People, fearful of what Catalina might do next, begin jeering at Calla and Katherine.

Calla and Katherine look at each other before they remember Asmi's advice: to turn the other cheek and to be honest with Catalina about how hurtful her behavior has been to the both of them.

Calla moves to get up and tell Catalina the truth about she feels about her, and Katherine almost stops her before remembering that Calla shouldn't do this on her own because she and Calla both have been victimized by Catalina.

"Catalina?" Calla asks, walking up to her rival with Katherine in tow.

"What do you freaks want?" Catalina inquires, putting on a facade.

"All we want to tell you is that everything you've done over the past two years has been really hurtful. I'm sure you see them as just jokes or pranks, but some other people may not take it that way – it may cause them to want to hurt themselves, or worse."

"Awww, someone's feeling brave today, isn't she? Listen here, missy, everyone would be better off if you just joined Hazel wherever she is."

"*I* wouldn't be, Catalina."

"Maybe you two should go down together, then."

"No. We won't let you treat us this way just because you're jealous I replaced you with someone who's actually nice to me!"

"Someone who's – now, see here, Katherine Griffiths, I was so incredibly nice to you! And our friendship didn't change until *she* came along." Catalina sneers, pointing her finger at Calla.

"I don't believe that you were nice to me before Calla started going to school here and living here. And you certainly weren't nice to Calla after she came around."

"I'm done talking to you, Katherine. You will rue this day. You will *all* rue this day!" Catalina shouts, storming out of the dining hall.

Once Catalina has left, Calla and Katherine move back to their seats.

"I can't believe I actually stood up to her, Katie. That *we* actually stood up to her."

"I'm proud of us, Calla."

"I am, too."

Soon, the beginning-of-the-school-year feast begins and all the parents, guardians and family members that can attend are in attendance. Queen Luana, however, is having a meeting with a visiting dignitary, so Nona is the visiting queen for the feast. As was said a couple of years prior, the visiting royals will be treated as equals, and not as higher-ups.

The children run forward to greet their families one by one, Katherine over to her dads Alex and Burton, and Calla over to her stepfather, Kit, and his girlfriend Inge.

"Calla! How's my big girl doing?"

"I'm fine, Dad."

"How's that arm of yours?"

"It still hurts, but it's getting better every day. Katie has been a huge help."

"I'm glad to hear that it's getting better, sweetheart. Now, shall we catch up with the others?"

"I think we shall, Dad."

Kit, Calla and Inge head into the school, and Inge, having never seen the inside of the school before, takes in her surroundings.

"Are we inside a castle, Calla? Why, this place is magnificent!"

"We are, Miss Inge. It is pretty beautiful, I must admit."

Calla and Katherine meet up and their parents say hello to one another. Nona soon arrives just as the students, faculty and family members are making their way into the dining hall.

"Nona! What a pleasure to see you again!"

"The pleasure is all mine, Kit."

"Where's Luana?"

"Oh, she had to go to a meeting with a visiting dignitary. Something that doesn't concern a consort. So, I'm afraid she won't be making it for the feast and the games and such."

"Well, tell Her Majesty she was dearly missed this evening."

"I will, Kit. Now, where's Emmalina? I do miss my daughter's hugs when she's away at school."

"Mum!" Emmalina spots her visiting mother and runs into her arms.

"Oh, my darling Emmalina! How I've missed you!"

"I've missed you, too, Mum."

"It's almost time for the feast to start." Calla announces as she approaches her cousin and visiting aunt with her sisters.

"Right. Let's get going to the dining hall, then."

The group makes their way to the dining hall and they sit down at the tables where their children are expected to sit with their year.

"Attention all parents, students, guardians, family members and faculty: welcome to this year's beginning-of-the-school-year feast. The main course this year, as usual, will be Hazel's summer stew, so please enjoy your fill, as the 10th years have worked hard to perfect her stew since her passing the summer of the previous school year.

"A salad of greens, cheese, and croutons will be the appetizer, while, after the main course, desserts will be served after the games have ended. Remember that everyone is welcome here, so no picking on anyone for any reason. And that goes for the parents, as well as the students."

Some people chuckle at this, but most remain silent, knowing that the main bullying victim right now is Calla.

Dinner is soon served, and everyone enjoys their food while chatting with one another.

"So, Calla, how are your classes going?" Kit asks his stepdaughter.

"They're going pretty well, thank you for asking, Dad."

"Anything challenging? I know you like a challenge when it comes to your schoolwork."

"Well, right now, everything is challenging because of my broken arm."

"Right. Is there anything I can do to help you feel more comfortable about your arm?"

"I don't think so, Dad, but thank you."

"You're welcome."

Meanwhile, Kazamir is near the school grounds, reporting to Qhuvelia.

"Catalina did as was commanded, m'lady. Now everyone knows that Calla Lilly is asexual."

"My plan is working perfectly, Kazamir. Soon, the girl's soul will be mine for the taking. I don't believe there's anything more for you to do before the holidays. But, during the holidays, I expect you to lure the girl to me, so the ritual can be complete."

"Of course, m'lady. Anything you need, I will try my best to provide for you."

"Very good, Kazamir. You are dismissed."

| 4 |

The Feast of the Goddess

Near the end of the calendar year, the students leave the School of the Seven Deities for the Feast of the Goddess. Emmalina invites her cousins, Calla, Victoria and little Celeste, their families, Calla's girlfriend Katherine, and Katherine's dads Alex and Burton to the Atteberry castle for the holiday.

Katherine and her dads are in awe of the castle, having never been inside before. The cooks and bakers are all busy preparing the seven-course feast while the royals get dressed in their finest gowns and suits.

Each course of the feast is designed to honor each of the gods and goddesses of Destiny: Sena, goddess of beauty, honoring her with a beautiful fruit salad as the first course; Era, goddess of time, is honored with fine aged wine for the adults and aged cheeses for the adults and the children; Nellie, goddess of healing, is honored with healing teas and fresh berries; Loana, goddess of wisdom, is honored with walnut-encrusted fish and chicken for those who don't eat or like fish.

Irah, god of nature, is honored with home-grown vegetables in a salad; Erik, god of magic, is honored with Hazel's summer stew, which can be enjoyed year-round and has just a pinch of magic; Aileen, the allmother, goddess of all humans and creatures, is honored with the final course: dessert, full of indulgent berries and rich chocolates.

Before the feast begins, everyone comes to decorate the weeping willow tree that takes up the majority of the foyer.

Asmi is running a little late, having just finished shopping for gifts for everyone, and Calla opens the door for them after seeing it's her Auncle Asmi.

"Calla, my favorite niece! How are you this beautiful morning?"

"I'm doing pretty well, Auncle. My arm has completely healed, thankfully."

"I am very glad to hear that, Calla. Now, be a dear and help me place the gifts near the tree so I can help decorate the tree and the castle."

Calla takes some of the gifts that her auncle is carrying and helps them put the gifts near the tree so the gifts won't be in the way of the royals and their guests decorating.

After putting some baubles and tinsel around the tree, Calla, her sisters, cousin, and girlfriend all get to work putting garland around the banisters of the staircases around the castle, all the while, soft holiday music is coming from a record player as everyone decorates.

Once the decorating is finished, everyone gathers in the formal living room so they can tell each other tales of years past.

The children have fun playing hide and seek while the adults chat, despite there being four teenagers in the group of children.

The following day, the Feast of the Goddess begins at noon.

The seven-course meal is served to all the waiting royals and their guests.

Queen Luana, as is tradition, says the prayer at the beginning of the feast. Everyone closes their eyes and puts their hands behind their back as the prayer is said.

"Oh, Aileen, goddess of all humans and creatures; Erik, god of magic; Irah, god of nature; Loana, goddess of wisdom; Nellie, goddess of healing; Era, goddess of time; and Sena, goddess of beauty, I pray to you yesterday, today, tomorrow and forever to honor the seven of you with this feast and to help it bring us pleasure and nourishment. By the power of the seven deities, so be it."

"So be it." The royals and commoners alike echo their queen.

Everyone begins conversing with one another as the food is being eaten.

"Emmalina, that gown you're wearing looks exquisite on you!" Asmi remarks.

"Thank you, Auncle Asmi. I – well, Mama and Mum – commissioned this gown for me as an early feast gift."

"How nice of Their Majesties to commission such a gorgeous ensemble. Speaking of the royals, Queen Luana, how are your parents enjoying their retirement?"

"They're both enjoying it quite well, Asmi, thank you for asking. Oh, I do hope they make it on time for presents."

"As do I, Your Majesty." Asmi replies.

Soon, each course has been served and eaten, and the royals and their guests join together to exchange gifts in the formal living room after Luana tells the origin story of Aileen, the allmother.

"The year is 2864, and there is utter chaos. It's the end of the world, and my great-great-grandfather King Graham Atteberry, and his wife, Queen Anne Lupton, are about to leave planet Earth for the dwarf planet Gnypso. Gnypso was founded on September 25, 2865, along with its countries Hartreusia, Lavenderia, Rosiary, Indigonia and Eburnean. But the story of Gnypso's founding is for another time.

"Aileen blessed us with creatures from all walks of life, and gave us the planet we have called home for at least the past 200 years. Aileen, the allmother, created Gnypso and sent out her sons and daughters – who were created by asexual reproduction – Erik, Irah, Loana, Nellie, Era and Sena, to help create the planet before my great-great-grandfather and his family and friends arrived.

"Erik, the god of magic, gave Calla's great-grandmother Hazel the power to create magic from yarn itself, and Aileen created magical sheep to make the wool for the yarn. Irah, the god of nature, gave life to all plants and animals, while Era, the goddess of time, made time slow down so the gods and goddesses could do their work in seven weeks, one week for each of the gods and goddesses. Nellie, the goddess of healing, helped Irah make medicinal plants and herbs and brews to help aid any sick or injured people or animals.

"Loana, the goddess of wisdom, planted seeds of knowledge in her brothers' and sisters' heads so they would each know exactly what to do, according to what their mother had instructed them to do. Sena was instructed to place all different kinds of plants, trees, mountains, hills and flowers all around the planet Gnypso, creating forests, mountain ranges, and fields of flowers. Once everything was completed, Aileen looked at all her children had finished for her, and she decided that everything was ready for the humans to arrive, thus her bringing about the end of the world. And that, everyone, is how Aileen created Gnypso for us."

Everyone claps and cheers at the end of the story.

"Now, it is time to hand out the gifts. Asmi, if you would be so kind." Luana tells Asmi.

"It would be my honor and my pleasure, Your Highness." Asmi replies as they do their bow-curtsy combination before going to the weeping willow to get some of the gifts for the children, so they can open their gifts first.

Once the five children have received their Feast of the Goddess gifts, they each open their presents. Emmalina receives a doll she had been admiring in a store window in Rosiary, the same doll her mother Nona had admired all those years ago before the fire at the tavern that had killed her parents. She also receives a new gown and some decorations for her room.

Calla, Victoria, little Celeste, and Katherine all receive books from the adults to read for their pleasure. Each of the children thanks Asmi and their family members for their gifts, and the adults tell the children that they're welcome.

The adults receive their gifts next, and they receive jewelry, clothes, and books, much to their liking.

The gift-giving soon ends, and the royals, their friends and families all sing Feast of the Goddess songs together, such as "Seven Courses of the Feast", "The First Feast on Gnypso", "Gods and Goddesses We Love", and "O Come All Are Grateful". These songs are all parodies of old Christmas songs from Earth: "Seven Courses of the Feast" parodies "Twelve Days of Christmas", "The First Feast on Gnypso" parodies "The First Noel", "Gods and Goddesses We Love" parodies "Angels We Have Heard On High" and "O Come All Are Grateful" is a parody of "O Come All Ye Faithful".

Once the singing ends, the children all head to bed with their bellies full and treasures galore, so the adults can have some champagne and talk amongst themselves.

After the children are in bed, a figure rushes to the breaker panel and turns off all of the lights.

Everyone screams before Luana steps up to the still-lit fireplace.

"Everyone, remain calm. Take out your phones and turn on the flashlight. Kit, Asmi, I'll assign the both of you to go check on the children."

"Right away, Your Majesty." Asmi replies.

"I'm hoping what's happening here isn't a repeat of my wedding day to Celeste." Kit murmurs to himself.

"We can always hope that that's not what's taking place here, Kit." Asmi responds as they and Kit walk up the stairs to the children's hallway of the castle.

"Asmi, you go check on Emmalina. I'll check on Calla, Victoria, Celeste and Katherine."

Asmi salutes Kit before walking to Princess Emmalina's bedchamber. They knock on the door before heading in.

"Princess Emmalina? It's your Auncle Asmi. Are you alright?"

"The lights have gone out, including my nightlight. I'm scared, Auncle Asmi."

"No need to be scared, little one. I will do everything in my power to protect you and the other children. Come on." Asmi holds out their hand for Emmalina to take.

Emmalina clings to her auncle, and the two walk to where the other children and Kit have gathered.

"Emmalina, stay with the other children. I'll secure the perimeter." Emmalina nods, and goes over to wait with her cousins and friend in Calla and Katherine's room. The children huddle like a crèche of baby penguins while Kit protects them as best he can while Asmi secures the area.

After Asmi has checked the bedroom, the bathroom, and the sitting room and closet, they rejoin the group, and they wrap a protective arm around Emmalina.

"Now what do we do, Dad?" Calla asks.

"We wait – we just simply wait, Calla."

"Okay."

Soon, Ciara, the royal page, knocks on the door of the suite, and Kit goes over to see who it is before opening the door.

"Who is it?"

"It's me, m'lord. Ciara, the royal page." Kit opens the door just a crack and sees that it is Ciara.

"What news do you bring, Ciara?"

"Well, sir, no one has been caught yet, but the lights are going to come back on very soon. I'll come and tell you when it's safe to come downstairs with the children."

"Thank you, Ciara."

"You're welcome, sir."

Ciara closes the door behind her and waits with the guards that have been posted outside the door.

Once the lights turn back on, and Ciara has given the all clear, the children, with Asmi and Kit, head downstairs to see if anything had happened besides the lights turning off.

"Queen Luana? Is anything the matter?" Kit asks as he and the children and Asmi make their way downstairs. Queen Luana is pacing in front of the fireplace in the formal living room, Nona looking at her wife worriedly.

"It's been stolen."

"What's been stolen, Your Majesty?" Asmi inquires.

"A million zikapia. I don't know why the thief didn't take more than that, but that's what was stolen."

"We must find the thief and apprehend them immediately!" Asmi exclaims, one for dramatics.

Emmalina shrinks back a bit, scared of what has happened: some of her parents' fortune has been stolen and no one knows who it was.

"Don't be scared, Princess Emmalina. We'll make sure you, the other children, and all of the adults that live and work here are safe." Asmi says, crouching down to Emmalina's level.

"Thank you, Auncle Asmi."

"You're quite welcome, Princess." Emmalina hugs her auncle and Asmi returns the gesture.

Once the excitement has died down a bit, the adults gather together while one of the servants watches the children. The adults want to figure out who had stolen the million zikapia. But little do they know that the children are planning on doing the exact same thing.

"We must figure out who is behind this theft as soon as possible!" Asmi pronounces.

"Agreed, Asmi. I say we round up the staff and interrogate them one by one."

"And I say we let the children interrogate them. Children can see through adults' lies...well, for the most part, anyway." Inge utters, speaking her mind.

"I agree, Inge. If that's alright with you, Your Highness." Kit observes.

"It's fine by me. I believe Emmalina should be the one to ask the questions, being the youngest."

"Agreed. Children?" Kit asks.

"Yes, Dad?" Calla answers.

"You, Emmalina, Celeste, Victoria and Katherine will be in charge of interrogating the adults to see who stole the million zikapia."

"Us? Why us?"

"Because you're children, and, for the most part, you can see through adults' lies."

"If all of you are sure, Dad."

"We are. And Emmalina will be the one conducting the interrogation to find the culprit."

| 5 |

Interrogations and Accusations

"What's a culprit?" Emmalina asks.

"Well, sweetheart, a culprit is someone who's done something bad – something illegal." Nona tells her daughter.

"I see. And you want *me* to do the interro-interrogations?"

"Yes, Emmalina. It must be you, and it must be done."

"Me? Why me?"

"Because you're the youngest *and* you're the crown princess, which means the adults may have a hard time lying to you, so they'll want nothing more than to tell you the absolute truth."

"Alright."

"Calla and Katherine will be with you throughout the interrogations to make sure the adults don't bully or harass you."

"What about me and Victoria?" Celeste asks.

"You two will be in charge of making sure the adults stay in line."

"Okay!"

"Let's get to it, then!" Calla exclaims.

The adults – royals, servants and commoners alike - are rounded up into a line, and Victoria and little Celeste are making certain that the adults don't go anywhere.

Emmalina starts the interrogations, starting with asking Luana questions.

"Mama, where were you this evening?"

"Well, Emmalina, I was in the formal living room telling stories with the other adults."

"Can anyone prove your whereabouts?"

"Well, I do believe anyone who was in the room can prove my whereabouts."

"Okay. I believe you. Next!"

Nona comes into the room and Emmalina interrogates her. Soon, Nona is dismissed and everyone in line has been interrogated – everyone but one person: Asmi.

"Auncle Asmi, where were you this evening?"

"Why, I was in the formal living room, of course. And, before you ask, lots of people can prove my whereabouts. Mostly the royals, but still people nonetheless."

"Alright. Please leave us so we can figure out who did it."

"Of course."

Asmi leaves, and, after they leave, the girls join together to see if they can figure out who had stolen the million zikapia.

"I do believe it wasn't anyone here...so who could have done it?"

"I'm not sure, Emmalina. But we must make a decision on who we say is guilty of the crime." Victoria says.

"There must be *someone* who had done it. But who?" Emmalina inquires.

"Well, one thing's for sure: we can't accuse someone who didn't do it."

"Agreed, Celeste." Calla tells her youngest sister.

"So, we're at a crossroads…and a crossroads that can't easily be walked…we're stuck." Katherine remarks.

The five children make their way out of the interrogation room and they face the adults.

"Well, children? Who's the culprit?" Kit asks.

"We have come to a decision and we've reached the conclusion that we have absolutely no clue who stole the million zikapia. Everyone we interrogated has an alibi, so we don't know who could have committed the crime." Calla announces.

"We're sorry we failed."

"Don't be, Emmalina. We shouldn't have put such a big weight on you children's shoulders." Luana tells her daughter.

The children look at each other misty-eyed as they realize they've failed.

"But we can't give up yet! We just *have* to figure out who did this horrible and heinous crime!" Emmalina exclaims.

"But there's no one left for us to interrogate, Emmalina."

"We haven't interrogated that person yet. Why can't we interrogate them?"

"What per-?" Calla stops talking abruptly.

Everyone in the hallway gasps as a hooded figure approaches them. They have a strange symbol tattooed on their right hand: a symbol that resembles a raven's head.

"Who are you, and how did you get in here?" Luana asks.

"Oh, I am no one in particular, but I am also everyone at the same time. I got in here because you left the front door open."

"Calla was the last one at the door after she helped me in!" Asmi exclaims.

"I must have forgotten to close it! Please don't hurt my family or friends. If you want someone to hurt, hurt *me* instead!"

"I want no harm to come to any of you. That's not in Qhuvelia's plan."

"Who's Qhuvelia?" Calla asks.

"Why, she's someone you can trust. The most trustworthy person to have ever existed."

The group before the hooded figure seems skeptical.

"Why should we believe you? And why are you even here?" Luana asks.

"Well, Your Majesty, I am here to tell you that someone among you stole the million zikapia."

"Who?"

"It was someone who seems trustworthy, but isn't really. But who that person is, is unknown to me, but is known to you all."

"So, was it one of the children?"

"Hard to say. Can anyone prove their whereabouts?"

"Emmalina was the only one alone in her suite."

Everyone looks at Emmalina accusingly.

"I didn't do it! Why would I steal from my own riches?"

"Because you don't have access to it until you turn 18, Emmalina." Luana scolds her daughter, not believing that her little Emmalina would commit such an inexcusable crime.

"And you're going to trust this unnamed stranger over your own daughter?" Emmalina asks.

"We don't really have a choice here, Emmalina. No one was with you in your room, and you know exactly where the breaker panel is so you could turn off the lights and commit the perfect crime. A crime that breaks your family's hearts." Nona says, tears welling in her eyes.

"I didn't do it, Mum! Honestly!"

"This stranger has no reason to lie to us. Calla, as an accessory to the crime, we're going to have to lock you and Emmalina both up in a heavily guarded cell until the morning. We'll interrogate you tomorrow." Luana states regally.

"Now, wait just a minute! Calla would never deliberately commit or be an accessory to any crime!" Kit argues.

"While that may be true, Kit, that doesn't excuse her at all! She may have accidentally left the door open all night, making it so Emmalina could sneak out and sneak back in without confrontation or anything, but she helped Emmalina unknowingly."

"I did no such thing!"

"You didn't even *know* that you helped Emmalina commit the almost-perfect crime, so there's no reason to argue, Calla. Guards!" Nona calls out.

"Yes, Your Majesty?" Matilde, Emmitt's sister and co-head of the royal guard, asks.

"Please escort Princess Emmalina and Lady Calla down to the dungeons and lock them up in separate and spaced out cells so they can't communicate with one another. We'll interrogate them in the morning."

"Your Majesty, are you sure? What crimes did they commit?" Richard, another head guard, asks, curiously.

"Emmalina possibly stole the missing million zikapia, and Calla was an accessory to her crime."

"Right away, Your Highness. Princess Emmalina and Lady Calla, if you'll please come with me."

"Dad, do something!" Calla calls out to her stepfather as she and her cousin are forcibly escorted down to the dungeons.

"I'll do everything I can to prove your innocence, Calla! I promise!"

Once the cell doors close on both Calla and Emmalina, the adults gather together worriedly, the hooded figure among them.

"This is an outrage, Luana! Locking up your daughter and my daughter for crimes they didn't even commit! It's unbelievable!" Emmitt says, temporarily forgetting his place as lord of Rosiary.

"I'm sorry, Emmitt, but what else were we supposed to do? Let the girls commit more crimes while we're sleeping?!" Luana asks.

"We don't even know for sure that *they* were the ones who committed the crime!" Kit exclaims, coming to Emmitt's defense.

"We're not sure that they aren't!" Nona states, coming to her wife's defense.

"We're getting nowhere! Those poor girls are locked up in cells, alone and scared, with no one to tell them that everything will be alright." Asmi says, coming to their nieces' defense.

"We've got to do something! Whether or not those girls are innocent, we can't just lock them up. What happened to 'innocent until proven guilty'?" Isabella asks.

"We need to get the story straight, and find out if Emmalina really committed the crime! We need to put pressure on her to make sure that we get the answers we need." Nona says.

"And what if the answers that we need convict both of the girls? We'd be without our princess for who knows how long, and we'd also be without our Calla." Asmi states.

"Emmalina is our daughter first, and a princess second." Luana counters.

"And yet you chose to believe a complete stranger over your own daughter!" Asmi argues.

"We're done talking about this, Asmi. Now, let's let everyone go to bed so we can deal with this in the morning." Luana reasons.

"Very well. I suppose it wouldn't do us *or* the girls any good to stay up and keep arguing." Asmi utters.

Everyone heads to bed, not noticing the hooded figure has since slipped out of the castle. The hooded figure makes their way to the Duskstrand on the outskirts of Hartreusia.

"Did they find out you were the one who stole the money?"

"No, Kazamir. They thought it was Emmalina and Calla."

"Good. Very good. Is the bag secure?"

"I've got it right here, Kazamir."

"That's why *you're* next in line should something happen to me."

"I still can't believe I pulled off the perfect heist! Alone, just me! And I got away with it!"

"I can't believe that those royals think their *precious Princess Emmalina and Lady Calla* committed the crime. You did an excellent thing there, Mya."

"Thank you, sir. But I have a question."

"Yes, Mya?"

"How will we get Calla to sell her soul to Qhuvelia? Surely, she won't trust you."

"Yes, but she won't trust *you* either, considering you were the one who started accusing her and Emmalina of the theft."

"So, who do we send out?"

"We'll have to go straight to the top."

"You don't mean - ?"

"Yes, Mya. We'll have to send out Qhuvelia herself. That is, if she agrees to do it."

"And what if she doesn't?"

"We always have someone else to send out, someone close to the royal family."

"Agreed. If Qhuvelia doesn't agree to be sent out to lure Calla, we'll send Asmi instead."

| 6 |

Apologies

While the royal family and their guests slumber, Calla and Emmalina are separately busy trying to figure out how to get out of this mess.

Calla is currently pacing in her cell, trying to figure out what to do, while Emmalina is sitting on the bed in her own cell, not doing much of anything but thinking about how to prove her innocence.

No one was there to see me go out or come back in after the switches in the breaker panel were turned off..but I know for a fact that I didn't turn them off or steal the million zikapia. Emmalina thinks to herself.

"I can't believe my own stepfather didn't do *anything* to help me," Calla says to herself.

The next morning, Calla and Emmalina are taken one by one to the interrogation room, where Richard and Matilde will be conducting the interrogations.

"May we get you anything, Lady Calla? Juice, water, soda?" Matilde asks.

"No. I just want to get out of here." Calla says with her arms crossed.

"We want nothing more than to make you as comfortable as possible, Lady Calla." Richard states.

"And how do I get to do that? Do I get to leave because I'm innocent?"

"No, Lady Calla, I'm afraid not." Matilde replies.

"Why do you call me 'Lady Calla'? I'm only a lady because of my birth father...okay, and my mother, as well. But still. No need to call me such things. I'm no lady, not properly anyway. I was only *born* into the position."

"It is royal protocol that the people we serve are addressed by their formal titles, Lady Calla." Richard counters.

"Can't we just keep it between the three of us?"

"I'm sorry, Your Ladyship, but we cannot change royal protocol. Her Majesty, Queen Luana, is the only one who can change that." Matilde answers.

"Let's just get this over with, then."

"Alright. It seems as if you did not close the door after your Auncle Asmi walked in with the Feast of the Goddess gifts. Any particular reason?"

"I must have forgotten to. I guess I could have kicked it closed, but that would seem rude to the other royals in my family."

"And, yet, you acted out in your youth: running away from home, secret trips to the site of the Indigonian manor explosion."

"Secret *trip*. Singular, not plural."

"My apologies, Lady Calla."

"Apology not accepted."

"As you wish, Your Ladyship. Next question: where were you the previous evening after the children received their gifts, and can anyone prove your whereabouts?"

"Yes. My girlfriend, Katherine Griffiths, can prove my where-abouts. I was in the guest suite with my girlfriend and we were reading to each other from the books we had received as gifts."

"So, you did not *intend* to be an accessory to theft?"

"No. And if you were smart – "

"I beg your pardon, Your Ladyship?"

"I *said* if you were smart, you wouldn't have accused Princess Emmalina and me in the first place...or listened to those that did. Not even Queen Luana and Queen Consort Nona."

"I must obey the queens unless it breaks royal protocol."

"And not believing the princess or a lady doesn't break royal protocol?!"

"No, Your Ladyship."

"Fine. Talk to Emmalina." Calla says before leaning forward in her chair to speak again.

"Just know that my stepfather will make sure you both pay for not being kinder to myself and to Princess Emmalina."

"We understand, Lady Calla. Matilde, if you would escort the lady back to her cell."

"What?! Back to my cell? I thought I was going to be set free, not jailed like some common criminal! If you want to catch any bad guys, catch Kazamir. He's the one you really want!"

"Kazamir has no connection to this case, Your Ladyship. Now, please, we will provide you with a lawyer, so we advise you not to speak any further."

"You're too late to give me a lawyer, for I've already told you all I know about this crime that I NEVER COMMITTED!" Calla screams.

"Matilde?" Richard inquires.

"Right this way, Your Ladyship." Matilde instructs.

Calla reluctantly is led back to her cell in the dungeons, and Emmalina is brought in for questioning.

"Princess Emmalina, may we get you anything at all? Water, soda? A snack, perhaps?"

"No, thank you, Captain."

"Very well. We'll get straight to the point: can anyone prove your whereabouts of last evening?" Matilde asks.

"Don't *you* usually stand guard outside my room, Matilde?"

"Yes, Your Highness."

"So how could I have snuck out at the late hour that I apparently did? There are guards posted outside all of my balconies, so there was no way I could have snuck out."

"We understand you're scared, Princess, but – "

"Are you questioning your future queen? Well, are you?"

"The only queens we answer to right now are your mothers. That won't change until you take the throne at 18, Your Highness."

"This is ridiculous! I didn't do it! I didn't steal the million zikapia! Why would I steal something that will be rightfully mine in less than a decade?"

"I – I guess you wouldn't, Your Highness."

"And you didn't answer my question."

"And what question was that, Princess?"

"How would I sneak out of my suite to commit the theft when every balcony is heavily guarded that is on either side of each window in every area of my bedchamber?"

"You wouldn't, Princess Emmalina." Matilde says, looking ashamed and realizing the mistake that's been made.

"And what exactly would I do with all that money I supposedly stole? I would probably keep it somewhere for safekeeping. Like, oh, I don't know, the royal vault? And I wouldn't have put it back in there because I don't know the combination or the code! Only my parents and grandparents know those things! And why would they tell me such things?"

"You make a good point, Princess." Richard states.

"And if I had sleepwalked, someone was bound to have caught me before I could have attempted to commit any crime."

"We apologize profusely, Princess Emmalina. We've made a horrible mistake believing the queens when we should have believed the child that hasn't told a lie since she was brought into the Atteberry family."

"Thank you for your apology, Captain and Co-Captain. I will think about forgiving you. And as for your behavior towards my cousin, Lady Calla..."

"Princess, we will do everything in our power to make it up to her, and to you. We promise."

"Good. Now release my cousin from her cell and escort us back upstairs at once. At once!"

"Right away, Your Highness." Matilde curtsies out while Richard bows out to go retrieve Calla from her cell and escort the lady and the crown princess back upstairs.

"What did you say to get them to release us?" Calla whispers to her cousin as they are escorted upstairs.

"Shhh. I'll tell you later, Lady Calla."

"Alright."

"We're very sorry for any trouble we may have caused for either of you young ladies. If there's anything we can do to make it up to you – "

"I want a dog."

"I'm sorry, Your Ladyship?"

"You heard me, Richard. I want a dog. And a gentle one at that, so it won't nip at or bite anyone. Playful, sweet, gentle and kind. Oh, and loyal, as well."

"I will see if I can arrange something to make sure you get a dog, Your Ladyship."

"I guess that will do for now, Captain."

Richard smiles softly and apologetically at the lady and the princess.

"And what would you like, Princess Emmalina? Would you like a dog as well?"

"Oh, no, Captain. What I want is to be queen for a day, to give me a taste of what's to come in less than a decade."

"We'll see what we can do to make sure that happens for you, Your Highness."

As soon as Calla, Emmalina, Richard and Matilde reach the main floor of the castle, they are bombarded with worried parents and family members and friends.

"Oh, Calla! I'm so sorry! I should have done more to prove your innocence." Kit says to his stepdaughter.

"As I should have done as well, Calla. You're my daughter as well, and I keep forgetting that. I may not be able to see your face, but I know that you're as beautiful as you're mother. And, yes, your mother was horrible at times, but she was kind towards the end of her life." Emmitt tells Calla.

"I forgive the both of you. All of you, really."

"We're glad to hear it. Now, how was the conclusion reached that Emmalina and Calla didn't commit the crime?" Luana asks queenly.

"Well, Your Majesty, Princess Emmalina actually reached that conclusion herself. There are guards posted outside on every balcony on the floor of her bedchamber, and in between each balcony is a window. Now, if the princess had sleepwalked, surely she would have been woken out of such a state before she could attempt to commit any crime, let alone a theft of one million zikapia."

"So, who do you think did it?"

"Actually, Your Majesty, we're not sure. We don't know if it's someone that's working as a double spy, or someone from the outside. We just don't know."

"And there's no one left to interrogate?" Nona asks.

"I'm afraid not, Queen Consort Nona. We've interrogated everyone that's been on the premises for the past few days. Now, to make it up to Her Highness and Her Ladyship, they've both decided what they would like as an offering for forgiveness."

"Captain, let me take a guess at what my stepdaughter wants. A dog, perhaps?"

"Y-yes, Your Lordship."

"Very well. But I expect this dog to be well loved and well taken care of, Calla. I will help you at times, but the sole care of the dog will go to you."

"Yes, Kit."

"And what did my daughter ask for?" Luana asks.

"You see, Queen Luana, Princess Emmalina asked to be queen for a day to give her – as she herself put it – 'a taste of what's to come in less than a decade'."

"I suppose we have no objections to her wish, considering that she was wrongly accused and her innocence has been proven." Nona says before looking at her wife Luana, who shakes her head in agreement.

"We will begin preparations for Her Highness' and Her Ladyship's wishes. Lady Calla, Lord Kit, would you both be so kind as to let me escort the two of you to the Rosiarian Animal Shelter, so that the dog would not have too far to travel from their former home to their new one?"

"I'm going, too! I would love to see if I can help Calla bond with her chosen pet. I do love animals and their companionship." Asmi says.

"Very well, Asmi. You may go as well." Richard says before turning to Matilde.

"Matilde, if you would be so kind as to help Their Majesties and Her Highness plan for her to be queen for a day?"

"Of course, Captain. I'll get started right away." Matilde replies.

Matilde and Richard both go off to separate parts of the Hartreusian castle to prepare for their separate tasks to make up the mistakes that were caused by them and the majority of the royal family.

| 7 |

Calla's Mental State

As preparations for the journey to Rosiary are underway, Asmi is searching for Kazamir, and they end up finding him in the garden once again.

"You know, I can't do all your dirty work for you." Asmi says, their hands on their hips.

"And get caught while you remain under the protection of the crown? Certainly not!"

"And you wonder why you're not the one in charge!"

"Neither are you!"

"I know that, Kazamir. Why did you want me?"

"In general or out here?"

"Out here, you imbecile. Don't think I don't know you're plotting to lure Calla away to sell her soul to Qhuvelia. However you do that is of no concern to me."

Kazamir sputters.

"And who told you that?"

"Like you, I have eyes and ears everywhere."

"But it *is* of concern to you, Asmi."

"Oh? How so?"

"If we don't get Qhuvelia to agree to come and lure Calla herself, she instructed that *you* do it instead."

"Why me?"

"Calla trusts you, does she not?"

"Yes, but – "

"But what?"

"Do you really want me to sacrifice almost a decade and a half of a relationship with my niece?"

"It's either that or you sacrifice *your life.*"

Asmi sighs.

"Fine, fine. But don't think of it as a favor to *you.* I serve only Qhuvelia."

"Very well. Go, then. See what you can do to lure Calla away from her family to here."

"That *might* be a problem."

"And why is that?"

"Because she and her stepfather, along with Richard and I, are going to Rosiary soon to pick out a dog for her to make up for accusing her of helping Emmalina steal a million zikapia from the Atteberry family's royal fortune."

"Do what you can to lure her away from her new companion, her stepfather and her guard."

"I will do as I have been asked."

"Good. Now go. Get out of here before someone notices you're missing."

Asmi mockingly salutes Kazamir before heading back to the Hartreusian castle.

"There you are, Asmi! We were wondering if you weren't going to make it!" Kit exclaims.

"And miss Lady Calla getting her first dog? I think not, Lord Kit!" Asmi says.

"Where were you, anyway, Auncle Asmi?" Calla asks.

"Well, Lady Calla, I was out in the garden."

"Taking in the scenery of Hartreusia before we leave?"

"That, and stretching my legs before the long journey. Now, Lady Calla, are you ready to go find your new best friend?"

"I already have a best friend."

"Yes, you do. But what I meant was 'are you ready to find your new companion, your new pet?' Things like that."

"I sure am!"

"Good. Lord Kit, do I still have time to bring my suitcases downstairs from my guest suite?"

"I had the servants do that for you."

"Oh, good. That way my back won't give out."

"We'll only be gone for about two weeks, Auncle."

"I know. But I like to be well-prepared. Shall we?"

Calla tries to contain her excitement as she, Asmi, Kit and Richard head to say their farewells to their family members.

"I do hope we'll be back in time to see you be queen for a day, Princess Emmalina." Calla says, curtsying to her cousin.

"And I do hope you'll make it a few days early so I can meet your new dog. Have you picked out a name yet, Lady Calla?"

"Not yet, Your Highness. I'm sure it'll come to me when I meet my new companion."

"Calla? We must get going." Kit calls.

"Coming, Dad!"

With one final curtsy, Calla leaves her aunts, cousin, and other friends and family members to go on the journey in search of her new pet.

As Asmi, Richard, Calla and Kit board the carriage bound for Rosiary, the other royal family members, along with Katherine and her two dads, wave goodbye to them as they leave.

It takes about a week to get from Hartreusia to Rosiary, and in that time, the group chats and plays card games with one another.

Once they arrive in Rosiary, Kit, Richard, Calla and Asmi head to the Morrison estate to unpack and settle in for the night, as they are all tired from their journey.

Once Calla has finished unpacking in her bedchamber, she eavesdrops on her stepfather talking on the phone with his girl-friend Inge.

"That wouldn't be wise, Lady Calla."

"Oh! Nanny Alison! I didn't hear you."

"There's a saying that goes 'some people are supposed to be seen and not heard'."

"Whoever made up that saying was a quack. I believe everyone should have a voice and an opinion...well, maybe not *everyone*."

"Oh?"

"Those with differing opinions on one's sexuality or gender identity...it's not any of that person's business, and should lie on the person alone who is going through figuring out their sexuality or gender identity, and even beyond that, when they've found out who they truly are."

"Wise words from a girl still so young. Lord Kit told me that you are here to adopt a dog from the shelter. He also told me about what happened with the door that had been left open, causing someone to come and steal a million zikapia from your cousin's and aunts' fortune."

"We still don't know who did it. I was hoping to get something of a tracking or hunting dog, so they could sniff for clues."

"Are you sure that's the kind of dog you really want? What about something small or something that's somewhat of a lap dog?"

"That would be nice, Nanny Alison."

"It was just a thought, Lady Calla. The only opinion that matters here about the situation is your own. Now, would you care to come with me to the kitchen to help the cooks get dinner ready for the family?"

"What are we having?" Calla asks as she and Alison start walking towards the kitchen.

"Hazel's summer stew."

Calla stops walking and backs up a few feet.

"Oh...I didn't know. On second thought, I'm not very hungry."

"Are you sure, Lady Calla? I'm sure we could find you something you'd like to eat."

"No, thank you, Nanny Alison. I'll just head back to my room and read for a while."

"Alright, then. If you change your mind, Lady Calla, give me a call."

"I will, Nanny Alison."

Calla heads back to her room, her nanny staring after her worriedly. Alison heads to where she'd usually find Kit, in his study.

"Lord Kit? May I speak with you for a moment?" Alison asks, lightly knocking on the door.

"Of course, Alison. How may I be of service to you?"

"You see, sir, it's Lady Calla."

"Is she alright? Is she sick?"

"No, sir, she's not sick. It's nothing like that."

"Then what seems to be the problem, Alison?"

"Well, sir, at first, she wanted to come and help the cooks prepare dinner for tonight. But once she heard you were having Hazel's stew, she said she wasn't hungry anymore."

"That's strange. Maybe she doesn't feel comfortable eating it without her."

"May I be honest with you, Lord Kit?"

"Of course."

"I believe, and please don't take this the wrong way, that Lady Calla has survivor's guilt."

"It *would* make a lot of sense. And I heard that it's a symptom of post-traumatic stress disorder. My little girl has survivor's guilt?"

"I believe so, Lord Kit. Lady Calla *was* there when Hazel sacrificed herself so Lady Celeste wouldn't be in any pain where she was."

"What do you suggest we do?"

"Well, I suggest a thorough mental and physical examination must be performed on Lady Calla."

"I see. It looks like we may have to cancel looking at dogs tomorrow, if my daughter's mental health is at stake."

"If I may, sir, depending on the severity of the mental illness, Calla may benefit from an emotional support dog, or even a service dog."

"I've heard of service dogs. Never had one myself, but I have heard of people having them. You really think a dog could help her?"

"Well, I don't know that for sure. And, if she does, in fact, need a service dog or an emotional support dog, I'm afraid a shelter dog won't do, unless it's highly trained to complete service tasks."

"I understand. You've given me a lot to think about, Allison. I suppose I should start with calling a local psychiatrist and physician to make appointments for Calla."

"That would be a wise thing to do, Lord Kit."

"You've convinced me. I'll call them now."

Alison nods and turns to leave before turning her head back towards the young lord.

"Is that all you'll need me for, for now, Lord Kit?"

"I believe so, Alison, yes. And thank you for your assistance and your honesty."

"You're welcome."

Alison smiles softly at the young father and leaves him to make the necessary phone calls.

After a quiet dinner with just Asmi and Kit, the two worriedly looking at Calla's empty chair, Kit heads upstairs with Asmi to have a brief but loving chat with Calla.

"Calla? It's Asmi and Dad." Kit softly raps on his stepdaughter's door.

"Come in." Asmi and Kit look at each other concernedly, both of them noticing the tears in Calla's voice. They enter, and they see that Calla is now face-down on her bed, all but sobbing.

"Calla? What's wrong, sweetheart?" Kit asks as he and Asmi sit on the edge of the bed.

"I – I'm broken."

"And what makes you think you're broken, pet?" Asmi asks their niece.

"Because I still feel guilty about Hazel."

"Calla...you may feel guilty about Grandma Hazel for a long time, but, eventually, the feeling might pass." Kit says.

"'Might'?" Calla asks, lifting her head up just a bit.

"If you don't talk to someone, the guilt will most likely cause you to do self-destructive things, like hurting yourself." Asmi says, truly concerned for their niece.

"But I don't *want* to hurt myself, Auncle Asmi."

"We know that, sweet pea, but sometimes, our mental illnesses, or even *physical* illnesses can become too much for us, and we want to be able to control our pain. But once we start hurting ourselves, we do more harm than good, and not just to ourselves, but to others as well." Asmi advises, caressing Calla's hair.

"What should I do?"

Asmi nods at Kit, who is prompted to tell Calla what needs to be done next.

"Well, sweetie, you should talk to someone. Alison observed that you might have survivor's guilt."

"What's that?"

"It means that you were a witness to someone dying and you didn't die yourself but you felt like you *should* have. The thing is, Calla, is that survivor's guilt is one of the symptoms of post-traumatic stress disorder, or PTSD."

"That sounds really scary."

"It can be scary, Calla. But we're here to help you through this and support you in any and every way we can. Tomorrow, instead of going to look for a dog, we're going to see a psychiatrist and a physician, to see if we can't get you properly diagnosed, and to see if you're in physical shape. But mental health is just as important as physical health, Calla." Asmi says.

"You both care about me that much?"

"Of course, Calla! We're your family, and no one should give up on or abandon their family."

"Will I be okay?"

"You will be with time, Calla. Won't you please come downstairs and get something to eat?"

"Okay."

"That's our girl." Kit takes his teenage daughter's hand and they start to head downstairs before realizing Asmi isn't following them.

"Auncle Asmi?"

"Huh? Oh, I'll be down in just a minute, Calla. I promise."

Calla nods at her auncle and she and Kit go downstairs to the kitchen to see what they can get Calla to eat.

Meanwhile, Asmi sits on the bed, on the verge of tears as they dial Kazamir's number.

"You better have some good news to report, Asmi."

"It can't be her, Kazamir. The child is already suffering enough as it is."

"And what's *that* supposed to mean?"

"She – she has survivor's guilt, which is a symptom of PTSD."

"So? Get her a counselor or a prescription or something. We can't have any delays in the process."

"It's not that simple."

"What do you mean?"

"PTSD has no cure, but it can be managed if taken care of properly."

"What do you mean PTSD has no cure?!"

"Unlike most physical illnesses, most mental illnesses have no cure. They can only be managed with counseling and sometimes medications."

"So, do what you must! And don't call again unless you have an actual report to give me."

Asmi sighs after they hang up the phone.

Getting Calla to Qhuvelia is going to be more difficult than Asmi thought.

| 8 |

Calla's New Friend

The following day, Calla, Kit and Asmi are in a psychiatrist's office, all of them ready for Calla's evaluation.

"Calla Morrison?" A nurse calls, walking into the waiting room.

"That's me."

"If you'll come with me, Miss Calla, and we'll get you measured, weighed and evaluated. Asmi, Lord Kit, please follow us."

"Okay."

Calla gets weighed, her height measured and her blood pressure and temperature taken.

"Everything looks good to me, Miss Calla. If you three will head back into the waiting room and the psychiatrist will call you in shortly."

"Thank you."

"You're welcome."

The three head back to the waiting room and sit down to wait for the psychiatrist.

Soon, Calla and Kit are called back for Calla's psychiatric evaluation.

"Good luck, Calla. I'll be right out here, waiting for you."

"Okay, Auncle Asmi."

"Please, Lady Calla and Lord Kit, take a seat."

Kit and Calla both take their seats in chairs next to one another in front of the desk where the psychiatrist is sitting.

"Now, Lord Kit."

"Please, just call me Kit."

"Alright, Kit. You called me yesterday, concerned for your step-daughter's mental health. You mentioned she's been experiencing symptoms of PTSD?"

"Yes, that is correct."

"Calla, do you have any objections to being evaluated for PTSD?"

"No. But I would like to know more about it."

"I will provide all the information I can for you about PTSD."

The psychiatrist begins talking about how PTSD can start and be diagnosed, and then she talks about the symptoms of PTSD, and the differences between C-PTSD and PTSD.

After Calla's evaluation is complete, the psychiatrist looks over her notes.

"Well, Calla, considering the fact that you've been experiencing survivor's guilt over the past 24 hours, it's definitely too soon to tell whether you have PTSD or C-PTSD. I will suggest, however, giving you a month to write down any flashbacks, nightmares or bad feelings you experience, either in a journal or on your phone's notes application. In a month, you can come back and I will have one of my coworkers that is a therapist evaluate you as well, and we can see if you have PTSD or C-PTSD, and we can work on getting you the proper treatment you need. Does that seem fair to the both of you?"

"Yes, ma'am." Calla says, Kit nodding in response to the psychiatrist.

"Very good. I'm sorry you've been feeling guilty about your great-grandmother's death, Calla, and I wish you the best and I hope to see you in a month."

"Thank you."

"You're welcome."

Kit and Calla leave the psychiatrist's office and head to the front to make a follow-up appointment. After the appointment is made, Calla, Kit and Asmi head to the healer's office next door for Calla's physical.

Waiting for the healer takes longer than the actual appointment, and the appointment is virtually painless for Calla.

"Miss Calla, I am very happy to say that you're in peak physical health. But your mental health, however, has been evaluated, correct?"

"Yes, sir."

"Good. I suggest coming back each year for a checkup. I wish you the best of luck with your psychiatric diagnosis, Miss Calla, and have a great new year. You are allowed to leave."

"Thank you, Healer Jones, for your help."

"You're quite welcome."

Calla, Kit and Asmi leave the healer's office, and head home.

On the way home, Calla, emotionally and physically exhausted from the day, falls asleep on her auncle's shoulder. Asmi and Kit look at each other worriedly before looking at Calla with the same expression. The two begin to speak in hushed tones.

"I'm worried for Calla, Asmi."

"As am I, Kit."

"What do you think we should do to help her within the next month?"

"Just make sure she doesn't harm herself. I'm not saying we have to watch her like a hawk, but I *am* saying that she doesn't need to feel alone. Remember, Kit, like my jerk of a father, I have eyes and ears everywhere."

"Will those eyes and ears be reliable?"

"They will if I have any say in it. I won't force them to do her any harm, but I will tell them to keep a watchful and gentle eye on Calla."

"We wouldn't want anyone to do her harm, Asmi. Right?"

"That is correct. I wish no ill will upon Calla or any member of my family, and that includes you, Kit. You may be her stepfather, but you were one of the ones who was there for her when she got her first period."

"It wasn't easy, Asmi."

"No one said it *was* easy, Kit."

"So, now what do we do?"

"We wait and evaluate Calla for the next month, and hope she writes down any bad feelings, flashbacks or nightmares."

"And if she doesn't?"

"Well, we can't *force* them out of the poor child."

"No, we can't. If she at first doesn't write down the flashbacks, nightmares and bad feelings, we'll gently and nicely ask her to do so for the remainder of the time before her next appointment with the psychiatrist."

"And what if she won't listen, Kit? You were a headstrong teenager once."

"As were you, Asmi."

"All I'm saying, Kit, is that we need to be patient with the girl. Make sure she feels comfortable talking about her feelings and troubles."

"I agree, Asmi."

The carriage suddenly stops, and Calla startles awake.

"What's going on?"

"We're not sure. Calla, stay in the carriage. We'll see what's going on."

"No, Kit. I – I should be the one to go out. You're her stepfather. She'll be crushed if she were to lose you."

"And she'd be crushed to lose *you*, Asmi."

A scuffle is suddenly heard outside the carriage, swords clanging and shields clashing.

"Calla, Kit, you both stay here."

"Asmi, no!"

But Kit and Calla are too late calling out for Asmi, as they've already stepped out of the carriage.

"Gentlemen, what quarrel do we have here?"

"You know why we're here, Asmi. We're here for the girl."

"Absolutely not. I will not give up my niece so freely to some bandits. Now, shoo, all of you. GO!"

Kit and Calla both startle, having never heard that tone or volume of Asmi's voice before.

The moment Asmi steps back into the carriage, they're wide-eyed and a little pale.

"A-Asmi?"

"The bandits – I don't want to frighten you, but, Calla, they wanted you."

"*Me?!*"

"I'm afraid so, my niece."

"Auncle Asmi, oh, what should I do? It seems like everyone is after me: Catalina, my own family and now these – these bandits?"

Asmi holds out their hands for Calla to take as they kneel before her.

"I'm not sure what you should do, Calla. But what I *will* tell you is that you are not alone. You never have been, and you never will be. There will always be someone looking out for you, be it a family member or friend on Gnypso or in the Broken Realm. I promise, Calla, we'll look out for you and we'll look after you." Asmi says as tears well in both their and Calla's eyes.

Calla collapses on the floor of the carriage, sobbing and scared. Her auncle wraps their arms around her, comforting her as best they can.

"I-I'm so s-s-scared."

"I know you are, Calla. We'll do everything we can to make sure you're right as rain in no time. You'll see. Alright?"

Calla nods against her auncle's chest, and they slowly get up and sit back in their carriage seats.

Once they're home, Asmi carries a sleeping Calla up to her room, Kit following closely behind.

Over the course of the next month, Asmi and Kit calmly and kindly but firmly remind Calla that writing down any bad flashbacks or feelings or nightmares she has will benefit her, because if she does, she'll be able to tell the psychiatrist what she's been going through, thus being able to give her a proper diagnosis of either C-PTSD or PTSD.

Some days, she doesn't have flashbacks or bad feelings or nightmares, except in the back of her mind, and, when she does, she remembers to write them down, even when she's returned to school and is in class.

Headmistress West knows of Calla's possible PTSD, and has informed the faculty that Calla may write down anything she experiences that would be cause for diagnosis. Whenever Catalina bullies Calla or gets to her for writing down "silly" things like bad feelings, flashbacks or nightmares, Calla talks to Asmi, her emergency family contact within the School of the Seven Deities.

Calla's PTSD diagnosis may cause the need for a service dog or an emotional support dog, depending on the severity of her PTSD, which will be evaluated in four weeks.

One day, after Calla's last class of the day, she and Katherine are walking past the kitchen when Calla suddenly is come over by a flashback. She collapses onto her knees, an anxiety attack forming.

"Calla!" Katherine follows her girlfriend to the ground, but not getting too close, having dealt with anxiety attacks before herself.

"Calla, what do I do?"

"Asmi." The name is barely above a whisper, but Katherine can tell what Calla is saying.

"Ashton!" Katherine calls out. Calla and Katherine's friend Ashton had been walking by when he spots the two on the ground.

"Is Calla alright, Katie?"

"Go get Counselor Asmi. They'll know what to do."

Ashton nods and runs as fast as he can to the counselor's office, rushing in.

"Asmi!"

"Ah, Ashton. What brings you to my office at the end of your school day?"

"It's Calla. I think she's having a flashback and an anxiety attack. Katherine instructed I come get you."

"Lead the way, Ashton."

Ashton and Asmi run fast through the halls, bumping into students and faculty, but ignoring their protests.

Soon, the two reach Calla and Katherine and Asmi kneels before their niece.

"Calla? I'm here, pet."

Calla doesn't respond.

Asmi, having been trained to handle Calla's anxiety attacks, gently takes her hands away from her chest and lightly holds them.

A gaggle of students and faculty alike gather around the three worried people and Calla.

"Easy, Calla. You're having another anxiety attack. We'll work through your flashback after you've calmed down a bit. Now, what

I want you to do is to take in some deep, slow breaths. Can you do that for me, Calla?"

Calla nods and begins taking in deep, slow breaths.

"Good. Keep going. Now, I want you to breathe deeply and slowly, in and out."

Calla does so, and, soon, her anxiety attack ends, and she collapses on her Auncle Asmi.

"That's our girl. Miss Griffiths, if you will accompany Calla and myself to my office?"

"Of course."

Asmi picks up the trembling Calla Lilly and carries her to their office.

"Katherine, be a dear and close the door for me, please, so we won't be disturbed." Asmi says once inside the office.

Once the door is closed, Asmi gently places Calla on the couch inside the office, and both they and Katherine kneel in front of Calla.

"Calla? Can you hear me? You're in the counselor's office at the School of the Seven Deities in Eburnean." Asmi calmly states.

"I – I can hear you, Auncle Asmi."

"Good. Very good. Now, do you want to tell me exactly what your flashback was about, and how it was brought on?"

Calla nods, and Katherine gives Asmi a notepad and a pen so they can write down everything Calla says.

"I – I was just walking down the hall after my last class, and I remembered that Catalina and some of my other schoolmates have been teasing me about Hazel's death. And once I remembered that, the flashback when Hazel sacrificed herself for me started. It only ended when you helped me through my anxiety attack."

"I see. Could Catalina have triggered you in any way?"

"I don't believe so, Auncle."

"You do know you'll have to report this to your therapist and your psychiatrist, right, Calla?"

"Yes, Auncle."

"Very good. Katherine, would you be so kind as to get Calla some water?"

"Of course, Auncle Asmi."

"Thank you."

Katherine walks over to the water cooler, grabs a cup and fills it with cool water.

"Here you go, Calla."

"Thank you, Katie."

"You're welcome."

Soon, Calla finishes her drink, and she looks at her auncle with tears in her eyes.

"Auncle Asmi? Am I ever going to get better?"

Asmi sighs.

"To tell you the truth, Calla, getting better from mental illnesses might take a lot longer than getting over a cold or a broken bone."

"I understand."

"Are you feeling any better?"

"A little."

"Do you think you're well enough to go to the dining hall with Katie? Or would you prefer to eat in here?"

"Honestly, I'd prefer to eat in here, but I know that facing my problems will do me a lot more good than not."

"That's our girl. If you need me during dinner, come to the front of the hall, where the faculty table is. Katherine, I appoint you to look after Calla, and make sure she isn't triggered like this again."

"I'm on it, Auncle Asmi."

"Good. You girls may leave."

The two girls leave hand-in-hand, Asmi smiling softly after them as they follow the two young women.

Asmi knows that they can't report back to Kazamir without an actual update about Calla, and it has to do nothing with her current mental state.

Once the three reach the dining hall, there's a quiet chatter as people turn to see Calla walking in late to the hall.

"You know where to find me if you need me, Calla." Asmi says, placing a hand on Calla's shoulder. Calla nods at her auncle before she and Katie take their seats at the 10th years' table.

"Calla, how are you feeling after your anxiety attack?" Ashton asks.

"I'm doing as well as I can, Ashton. Thank you."

The students and faculty are all served their food, and they begin eating. Once dinner ends, Calla and Katherine walk hand-in-hand to their dorms, where they call Kit to give him an update.

"Is that my favorite stepdaughter and her girlfriend?"

"Yes, Dad."

"Asmi mentioned you had an anxiety attack after a flashback. How are you doing, Calla?"

"I'm doing okay, Dad. I could be better, but I could be worse."

"I'm glad you're doing okay, Calla. Asmi also told me they wrote down what you said in regards to your latest flashback."

"They did?"

"Yes. Don't be cross at them, Calla. They're only trying to help you, like I am."

"I understand, Dad."

"Good. I'll see you in a few weeks to pick you up for your appointment, okay?"

Calla nods.

"Love you, Dad."

"I love you, too, kiddo. Good night, you two."

"Good night."

Calla hangs up the video call and sits back on the couch, Katherine following her lead.

"How are you, really, Calla?"

"I'm exhausted."

"So why didn't you tell that to Kit?"

"Because he'll never understand, Katie."

"Why wouldn't he understand? He lost Hazel, too."

"Yes, but he's not the cause of her death! He has no guilt to be ashamed of."

"You don't know that he doesn't feel guilty about leaving us alone, Calla."

"And *you* don't know that he does. I'm going to bed, Katie."

Calla gets up abruptly, and storms off to the bedroom.

"You shouldn't go to bed angry, Calla!" Katie calls after her girlfriend.

Katie sighs before breaking down. She doesn't know how to feel or what to do to help her girlfriend get better.

Once Katie has stopped crying, she, too, heads to bed.

"Calla? I'm sorry for assuming anything about Kit. You know him better than I do." Katie whispers to Calla, who's back is facing towards Katie.

Calla turns around to face Katie, and Katie sees tears streaming down her girlfriend's cheeks.

"What if I never get better, Katie? What if I'm stuck having flashbacks and anxiety attacks forever?"

"We'll get through this, Calla. You're not alone."

"I feel alone."

"You may *feel* alone, but that doesn't mean you *are* alone."

"I'm tired, Katie. I'm going to go to sleep, and I suggest you do the same."

"Alright, Calla. I – I love you." Katherine confesses.

"You do?"

"I do. It's alright if you don't feel the same way just yet. I just wanted you to know that I do love you."

"No...I *do* feel the same way, Katie. I love you, too."

"Y-you do?"

"I do."

"I'm glad to hear it. Let's never fight again, alright, Calla?"

"I agree. I hate it when we fight, Katie."

"As do I. Good night, Calla."

"Good night, Katie."

The two head off to sleep with their classmates all around the room.

By the time the next few weeks are up, Calla is physically, mentally and emotionally exhausted.

Calla and Katie say their goodbyes to one another before Asmi escorts Calla to the carriage where her stepfather is waiting.

"I wish I could go with you, Calla. But if any of the other students need me." Asmi starts.

"I understand, Auncle. Thank you."

"You're quite welcome. Send me updates, alright?"

"I will. Love you, Auncle Asmi."

"I love you, too, Calla."

Calla boards the carriage and hugs her stepfather before sitting across from him so they can ride to Rosiary together.

"Katherine told me you've been exhausted lately. Why didn't you tell me that when we spoke all those weeks ago?"

"Why didn't you let me call you during these last few weeks?"

"We'll get to that later, Calla."

"I didn't tell you because I didn't want you to feel ashamed of me, and because I don't want to feel like a burden to you."

"Oh, Calla. You're not a burden. You never have been and you never will be."

"I'm not?"

"No, and, for the record, I could *never* be ashamed of you."

"Really?"

"Really, Calla. Now, as for me not letting you call me over the past few weeks, I did so because I didn't want to spoil the surprise waiting for you at home."

"Can I have a hint?"

"I'm afraid not, sweetheart. I wouldn't want you to get too excited."

"Oh, okay."

"I'm sure you'll love the surprise, Calla."

"I believe you, Dad."

Soon, the two reach Rosiary, and they head straight to the psychiatrist's office.

"We'll be waiting out here for you both, m'lord and lady. And good luck, Lady Calla." The carriage driver says.

"Thank you."

"You're welcome."

Kit and Calla walk into the psychiatrist's office and check in.

After Calla gets her vitals taken, she heads back into the waiting room to wait with her stepdad.

Soon, the psychiatrist arrives to take Calla and Kit back to discuss the last month. Calla's new therapist is waiting in the office.

"Calla Lilly, have you written down all that you could about your bad feelings, flashbacks and nightmares?"

"Yes, ma'am."

"Good. May I read them?"

"Of course. One of them is on paper, while the rest are on my phone."

"I understand, Calla."

Calla hands the psychiatrist the paper and her phone, which is open to the notes app filled with flashbacks, nightmares and bad feelings.

The therapist and psychiatrist look over the notes and write down some notes of their own.

Soon, both the therapist and psychiatrist look at Calla and smile solemnly.

"Well, Miss Calla, it has officially been a month since we first monitored your symptoms, and it turns out that you have PTSD."

"I do?"

"Yes. We can start with either a medication or see if you qualify for a service dog. Now, Kit, may I tell her your news?" The psychiatrist asks.

"Of course."

"Calla, you may qualify for a service dog."

"What does that mean?"

"It means that your PTSD is unmanageable enough for you to get a service dog. Your stepfather carefully chose a dog for you, and, with your permission, we will hire some trainers to help train your dog to become your service dog, so that this dog can help with your PTSD."

Calla looks at her stepfather excitedly, but a little worried.

"You really got me a dog, Dad?"

"I sure did. But, like I've said, that dog is *your* responsibility, Calla."

"Yeah, Dad, I get that. I really get to have a dog?"

"Not just a dog, but a *service* dog, a dog that will be trained to help you with your PTSD symptoms. We'll have the trainers ride over with you to your estate so training can begin over the weekend. I assume you brought your homework with you, Calla?"

"Yes, ma'am, I did."

"Good. Because, in between training, you'll need to finish up your homework."

"I will. Wait, does this mean that my service dog can accompany me to school?"

"It sure does."

"Cool!"

"It's very cool, but, remember, Calla, a service dog is a lot of work, and it takes a lot of training for the dog to perform tasks specific to your disability."

"I'll work very hard to help train my service dog."

"We don't doubt it, Calla. Judith, Lionel?"

"Yes?" Two people walk into the psychiatrist's office.

"This is Calla. She'll be helping train her new service dog with you."

"It's a pleasure to meet you, Lady Calla, Lord Kit." Judith says, curtsying as Lionel bows.

"It's a pleasure to meet you both as well."

"Well, Calla, shall we be off?"

"I believe so, Dad."

"Let's go, then."

Calla, Kit, Judith and Lionel, with Judith's and Lionel's bags in tow, board the waiting carriage for the Morrison estate.

| 9 |

Asmi's Betrayal

Once the group arrives at the Morrison estate, Calla is welcomed with open arms.

"Welcome home, Lady Calla. There's someone who wants to meet you." Inge, Kit's girlfriend, says.

"There is?"

"Alison?" Inge calls. Alison walks forward with a Cavalier spaniel on a leash. The dog looks calm but excited at the same time.

"This is your new service dog, Calla, and it's up to you to name her."

"I think I'll call her – Faith."

"A great name for a great dog. Try calling her to you, Calla." Alison drops the leash and Calla kneels in front of her new service dog.

"Come here, Faith!" Calla calls. Faith immediately trots over to her new handler and Calla allows Faith to sniff and lick her hand to get to know her.

"Very good, you two. Now, I know you're all tired from your journey, so we've got dinner ready and waiting for you." Alison says.

"Thank you. What are we having?"

"Well, we're having roast chicken with potatoes and asparagus."

"Yum!" Calla says, causing everyone to chuckle at the young lady's enthusiasm.

The group heads into the estate, and they settle in around the table in the formal dining room. Faith loyally goes under Calla's chair.

Once dinner has been served and eaten, Calla and Kit head upstairs with Faith to see that a brand-new dog bed has been placed near one of the sides of Calla's bed. Faith goes to it with a little prompting from Calla. After circling in her bed a little, Faith settles down, but staying awake should Calla need her for anything.

After Calla has gotten ready for bed, she settles in bed with Faith in her own bed.

"Good night, Calla. Good night, Faith."

"Night, Dad."

Kit leaves the room and Calla caresses Faith's belly to give her comfort, and Faith relishes in the love from her new handler.

The next day, Saturday, Kit, Calla and Faith meet the trainers outside in the backyard to start service dog training.

"Now, Calla, as you're a spell caster, you must use your magic around Faith so she'll get used to being around you and other spell casters." Judith says.

Calla nods at Judith.

"What spell should I use?"

"You can use any of the ten spells, but I would suggest not using one that would be used in battle."

"Okay."

Calla whispers "Excuse Me" into her palm while holding Faith's leash. Everyone parts to make room for Calla and Faith, letting them pass by without question.

After a few spells are said by Calla, and they are performed, the group moves inside so Faith can learn more about how to turn on and off most of the lights in the estate, along with touching her nose or paw to Calla whenever Calla starts showing signs of anxiety or discomfort, Deep Pressure Therapy, or DPT, where Faith will lie down either on Calla's lap or her legs to bring her comfort. Faith will also perform the task of waking Calla up during nightmares, as well as circling around Calla so she'll have space to walk in a crowd.

Faith will also learn and perform the task of hugging Calla to bring her more comfort, but Calla must kneel down for this task to be performed.

Once training is complete, Calla and Faith are watched carefully by Judith and Lionel to make sure all the tasks are completed correctly by both Faith and Calla, and that Faith is rewarded fairly and often for completing said tasks by feeding her treats of dog biscuits, and sometimes pieces of cheese or a banana.

After Calla and Faith are both watched carefully by the trainers, Judith and Lionel are impressed by both Calla's and Faith's performance as a team.

After around a year and a half passes since the beginning of training, Calla is in her last year at the School of the Seven Deities.

Kazamir is not pleased with Asmi, nor is he pleased that it is taking so long to lure Calla to Qhuvelia.

"Do what you must to lure that mangy mutt away from Calla so the ritual can be done."

"Faith isn't just Calla's dog, Kazamir, she's also her *service* dog, so luring the dog away from her handler won't be particularly easy."

"I don't care what you have to do to separate them. Just do it."

Asmi sighs before leaving their secret meeting with Kazamir.

A few weeks pass from the beginning of the school year, and everyone – students and staff alike – have all gotten used to having Faith around as Calla's service dog, and they know not to touch or interact with Faith when she's working.

"Good afternoon, Miss Calla." Headmistress West says as she approaches Calla and Faith. Headmistress West ignores Faith, as is protocol for service dogs. Unless Faith is sent by Calla to get someone to help her, the dog is ignored by everyone, even Catalina.

"Good afternoon, Headmistress West." At 17 years old, Calla is the spitting image of her mother, and looks more and more like her every day.

"Are you ready to graduate this school year?"

"Yes, ma'am. I can't wait to officially become a lady of Rosiary."

"I expect to be in attendance, considering I helped you become a proper lady over the years."

"Yes, ma'am. I'd be delighted to have you there as I become a lady."

"I'm really looking forward to it."

"Calla? May I speak with you for a moment?"

"Yes, Auncle Asmi!" Calla calls back to her auncle.

"I really must be going, Headmistress West."

"Thank you for the brief chat, Calla. I really appreciate it."

Calla turns and she and Faith head to where Asmi had called her.

"Ah, Calla. Good to see you, dear."

"You wanted to see me, Auncle Asmi?"

"Yes, I did."

"What is this all about? Faith, leave it." Calla instructs, as Faith has been growling at Asmi, which she didn't used to do. The service dog quiets and sits at her handler's feet.

"Calla, would you mind walking with me? Your classes have finished for the day, correct?" Asmi asks.

"Yes, Auncle. But I don't understand."

"You will soon enough."

Asmi leads Calla – and Faith – to a forest on the outskirts of the School of the Seven Deities.

"If you would please step forward, Calla."

"What's going on?"

"Faith, come."

Faith doesn't leave her handler's side.

"Faith, go to Auncle Asmi. If I can trust him, so can you."

Faith cocks her head at her handler's instructions, but goes to Asmi after being prompted by Calla.

"That's a good girl, Faith." Asmi says, petting the dog's fur before turning their attention back to Calla.

"Step forward, Calla, and you will truly see why you're here in this forest of Eburnean."

"I trust you, Auncle Asmi."

"You made a horrible mistake trusting me, child. Didn't you know I've been working for Qhuvelia this whole time?!"

Calla gasps and Faith starts growling once again, then she barks over and over again before Asmi firmly but gently clamps Faith's muzzle shut with one of their hands.

Chanting in an ancient language begins as smoke surrounds Calla, Asmi at the lead, Kazamir by their side. Calla turns this way and that, trying to figure out what's going on.

"I've waited a long time for this, Calla Lilly Morrison." Kazamir says menacingly.

Once the chanting stops, a figure made of smoke and ash appears before Calla.

"Calla Lilly, you're here at last."

"Who – who are you?"

"I am Qhuvelia, goddess of the underworld, and I am here because your soul will belong to me. Kazamir, Mya, restrain the girl."

"Yes, m'lady." Kazamir and Mya both restrain Calla. Faith is tied to a tree nearby and Asmi put a spell on her to quiet her, with them using dark magic to do so.

"Asmi?"

"M'lady?"

"You know what to do."

As the chanting begins again, Asmi walks in front of Calla.

"Asmi, don't do this. You're family. *I'm* family."

"We may be flesh and blood, Calla Lilly Morrison, but that doesn't mean I consider you family."

"But you've helped take care of me for as long as I can remember."

"It was all a ruse, a trick, a scam. Whatever you want to call it, I am betraying you because I never felt like family in your home, or in your heart."

"That's not true! You can come back from this! We can walk away from this together, Asmi. Please! Don't do this."

But Calla's pleas fall on deaf ears.

"Don't bother begging, Calla. It'll only make it that much more painful, and not just for you."

The chanting continues and Asmi takes out a dagger, and they cut a slit in Calla's left hand.

Calla grimaces at this unexpected and painful gesture from Asmi.

"Don't make this harder than it has to be, Calla." Asmi tells Calla.

"Bring her to me, Asmi, then the ritual shall be complete."

Kazamir and Mya behind Calla, with Asmi dragging Calla by her arm, they go to Qhuvelia, and a drop of blood falls on Qhuvelia's skin and is absorbed by Qhuvelia.

"The ritual is finished. Your soul now belongs to me, Calla Lilly Morrison." Qhuvelia turns to Asmi, Mya and Kazamir.

"Let her and her little dog go. No one but Calla and her dog shall know of or speak of this afternoon." Qhuvelia says in a whisper.

Smoke rises from the depths of the underworld and surrounds Qhuvelia, Asmi, Kazamir and Mya. Once the smoke disappears, so, too, do Qhuvelia and her minions.

| 10 |

The Royal Decree

"Hmmm..." Calla groans as Faith licks her aching hand where Asmi had cut a slit into it.

"Faith, go get help." Calla says weakly, barely able to pick her head up.

Faith barks and runs as fast as her little legs can carry her back to the school. Faith's leash had been broken by Faith, and her leash is still tied around the tree.

Faith barks all the way to the school, and she finds Katherine talking with Headmistress West. She barks, whines and turns in circles after she gets to Katherine and Headmistress West.

"What is it, Faith? What – where – where's Calla?" Katherine asks. Faith barks and circles again, and then runs towards the direction of the forest.

"Run, Katherine! I'll catch up with you!" Headmistress West exclaims, gathering up her skirts. Katherine nods at the headmistress and they both follow Faith to where Calla is in the middle of the forest.

"Calla!" Katherine says, kneeling before her unconscious girlfriend.

"Oh, dear." Headmistress West mutters, kneeling as well.

Faith whines and licks at her owner's face, trying to bring her back to consciousness.

Soon, Calla starts to stir and wakes back up.

"What – what happened?" Calla asks groggily.

"You poor dear. You must have fallen and hit your head. But, Calla, wherever did you get that unsightly gash in your hand?" Headmistress West asks, placing a gentle hand on Calla's shoulder.

"It – it was Asmi."

"Asmi? The school counselor? Why, that's impossible!"

"They lured me here. They lured me to Qhuvelia and Kazamir."

"Qhuvelia?" Katherine asks, confused.

"The goddess of the underworld, Katherine." Headmistress West informs before helping Calla sit up.

"We'd better get you back into the school to see Nurse Morgan. Can you walk?" Headmistress West asks.

"I think so, Headmistress West."

"Good. Let's get going, then."

Headmistress West and Katherine both help Calla stand and they lead her to Nurse Morgan's office.

"I'll get you fixed up in no time, Miss Calla. Please, take a seat." Nurse Morgan says, leading Calla, Faith and Katherine back behind a curtain.

"Headmistress, if that will be all."

"Yes, Nurse Morgan. Thank you for taking care of Calla."

"You're welcome."

Headmistress West leaves Nurse Morgan to help heal Calla's wounds.

"This may sting a bit, dear." Nurse Morgan says, placing a salve over the gash on Calla's left hand.

Once the salve has dissolved into the gash and a bandage is wrapped around Calla's injured hand, Nurse Morgan sees to her other injuries.

"So, what exactly happened to you, Miss Calla? A bit too much playtime in the forest?"

"No, ma'am. What happened was that Asmi, my auncle, they tricked me into following them into a forest on the outskirts of the school." Calla continues telling her story to Nurse Morgan, and, by the end of it, Faith has put her head on Calla's foot to bring her some extra comfort.

"Well, I'm very sorry you went through that. At least Asmi didn't tell you that selling your soul to Qhuvelia would bring your Great-Grandma Hazel back."

"What?!" Calla and Katherine exclaim.

"It's not true, of course. No one can or should bring back the dead, even if it would make one feel less guilty for their actions."

"So, now what do I do?"

"I suggest taking it easy for a few days. Have Katherine turn in your homework while you recover here. I'll let you go in the morning, and I'll have one of my assistants bring you food and drink."

"Thank you, Nurse Morgan."

"You're welcome, Miss Calla. Now, just lay back. I'll see to it that something is brought in for your dog to do her business nearby, and one of my assistants will clean it up for you."

"Alright."

"That's a good girl. Katherine, could I speak with you for a moment?"

"Of course, Nurse Morgan."

Katherine and Nurse Morgan go behind a curtain to where the waiting room is and begin to speak in hushed tones, but Calla and Faith can both hear their conversation.

"Has Calla ever lied about something so serious, or would she? Maybe she hit her head so hard she doesn't know what really happened."

"No, ma'am. She'd never lie about something like this."

"Just making sure we don't need to get Calla's head examined more thoroughly."

"You don't believe me, Nurse Morgan?" Calla asks through the not-so-thick curtain.

"I do now, Calla. Believe me."

"Oh, alright."

Calla lay back in the bed in her section of the nurse's infirmary, Faith jumping up to lay next to her owner and handler.

Soon, Calla falls asleep with her loyal service dog Faith by her side, wondering what will come next for them.

~.~

The next morning, Calla wakes and stretches before remembering where she is. She sees Faith snoozing away beside her before getting out of bed and gently waking her service dog.

"Faith. It's time to get up." Calla says as she scratches Faith behind her ears. Faith yawns and stretches herself before getting up to follow her owner.

"Good morning, Miss Calla. How are you feeling today?" Nurse Hanna asks.

"Good morning, Nurse Hanna. I'm feeling pretty good. Thank you for asking."

"Are you ready to head back to the land of the awake?"

"Yes, ma'am."

"Good. Off you go, then."

Calla and Faith leave the infirmary and head off to breakfast. It's Saturday, so students are allowed to do as they please, within reason and within the school grounds.

Calla sits at the 12th years' table as she usually does for her last year here, and Faith sits under the table, out of the way of anyone.

"Calla! You're back!" Katie says, excited to see her girlfriend up and about.

"I'm glad to be back, Katie. What's for breakfast?"

"Anything we want. We're in year 12, you know. We can have cereal, donuts, fruit, bagels, waffles, pancakes, coffee, tea, hot chocolate – "

"Katie, I get it! I get it!" Calla says, laughing. Katie laughs along with her girlfriend before taking her bandaged hand.

"How's your hand doing?"

"It's doing alright, I guess. Katie, do people really not believe that Asmi did this? That I was forced to sell my soul to Qhuvelia?"

"It's hard to say, I guess. People *do* talk, love. But what exactly they talk about isn't exactly easy to find out."

"I understand. Let's eat. I'm famished!"

"You said it, Calla."

The two begin eating with the rest of their schoolmates, and, soon, breakfast ends and the students can leave the dining hall to do as they would like.

Calla and Katie, with Faith in tow, head to the school's library to catch up on homework and get some reading for pleasure in.

Once they reach the library, they settle in for a few hours to get some work done.

While there, Calla's tablet dings with a message from Kit, so she and Katie quietly read the message together. It reads:

"Calla, Headmistress West told me about what happened with your Auncle Asmi. I'm very sorry that that happened to you, and I know I will do everything in my power to make sure your soul belongs to Aileen once again, and not to Qhuvelia. Love, Kit (Your Stepfather)."

"I should probably write him back." Calla whispers as quietly as possible, but loud enough so Katie can hear her.

"Agreed, Calla. You wouldn't want to keep your stepfather waiting."

Calla types out a message, spellchecks it, and sends it to her stepdad. The message reads:

"Dad, Thank you for your message, it meant a lot to me. By the way, Katie says 'hi'. I hope we can restore my soul so it's Aileen's again. Love you, Dad. Love, Calla (plus Faith and Katie)."

Back in Rosiary, Kit is frantically writing a letter to Their Majesties, trying to see if any arrests can be made of Asmi, Mya and Kazamir.

After writing the letter to Queen Luana and Queen Nona, Kit brings it to the Morrison's personal mail carrier to bring it to Castle Atteberry as soon as possible.

"I'll get this to them right away, Your Lordship."

"Thank you, Gerard."

"You're welcome."

With one final nod, Gerard leaves the Morrison estate for the post office in the village of Lippin, so the letter will then be taken all the way to Hartreusia, on the other side of Lavenderia.

Once it reaches Hartreusia, Harold, the Atteberry's royal messenger, takes the letter (and the other mail) from the post office and heads back to the castle.

"Your Majesties? You have a letter from the Morrison estate in Rosiary."

"Please bring it here, Harold." Luana instructs regally.

Harold brings the letter to Queen Luana, along with the other mail, and places them in her lap.

"Thank you, Harold. Will that be all?"

"Yes, ma'am."

"Very well. Dismissed."

Harold bows out and heads back to his post.

"Luana, dear? Is that the letter from Kit?" Nona asks her wife as she approaches her from the other side of the dining hall.

"Yes, Nona."

"What does it say?"

"Let me see." Luana tears open the envelope with a letter opener and reads the letter. Her eyes go wide as she scans the contents of the letter.

"Well, Luana? What does it say?"

"It says that Calla was forced to sell her soul to Qhuvelia, the goddess of the underworld, and that Asmi was a part of it."

"Asmi? *Our* Asmi?"

"I'm afraid so, Nona. Richard?"

"Yes, Your Highness?"

"Please post a notice throughout the kingdom, and spread the word throughout the other countries of Gnypso. Tell the people that we are looking to arrest our former royal advisor Asmi, as well as Kazamir and one of Kazamir's bandits called Mya."

"Right away, Your Majesty." Richard leaves before gathering the rest of the royal guard and posting notices throughout the kingdom and suggesting the other royal houses do the same.

| 11 |

Securing the School

Once the decree is sent out regarding the arrests that must be made of Asmi, Kazamir and Mya, and anyone associated with them, the School of the Seven Deities is placed under lockdown until the arrests can be made. No one is allowed on or off of the school grounds until the royal guards have arrested mainly Kazamir, Asmi and Mya.

The students gather in the corridors, classrooms and the dining hall as normal, wondering if this is all a big misunderstanding or a prank. All eyes go to Calla, whom they believe is the cause of all of this.

Calla tries her best to ignore the stares and the glares she receives from her schoolmates, but her sisters, cousin and friends are there for her, to make sure she doesn't become self-destructive.

Faith is careful not to get underfoot of anyone as she follows her owner/handler through the corridors, the dorms, and the class-rooms.

The spell casters of the school all gather together to cast "Abra-cadabra" around the school to make sure nothing and no one can get in or out for the time being.

They gather and huddle in groups in the courtyard/quad, making sure that the nonspellers are standing back aways from them. With the exception of Calla, each spell caster takes out their ball of yarn and whispers "Abracadabra" into their palm, blowing on the spell and casting it around the school grounds, making sure that the school cannot be attacked by anyone or anything.

Once the spell casters have completed the spell, they breathe a sigh of relief, confident in themselves and their abilities.

The students and faculty all go about their business as they each make sure that the spell is intact for as long as possible.

Calla and Faith are walking in the corridors, just going about their day, when Calla starts feeling a bit dizzy. Faith paws at her handler, trying to get her to sit down before she passes out. Calla listens to Faith and sits down on the floor with her head between her knees to make sure she doesn't pass out, or, if she does, that the impact isn't too harsh.

When Calla looks up, no longer as dizzy, she sees Catalina, of all people, kneeling in front of her.

"Are you alright, Calla?"

"What do you care?"

"Well, Calla, as it seems, you and I are in the same boat."

"I'm tired of your games, Catalina. Just tell me."

"Calla, I heard that you were forced to sell your soul to Qhuvelia."

"How did you know about that?"

"Everyone knows about it." Catalina says, moving to sit next to Calla on the floor. Faith sniffs Catalina's hand before licking it lovingly.

"I think Faith likes you."

"We are cousins, after all."

"We are?"

"Yes. Kazamir is both your grandfather and mine. We have different grandmothers, though, so, technically, we're *half*-cousins."

"What were you saying before?"

"I was saying that you sold your soul to Qhuvelia unwillingly...as did I."

"*You* sold your soul to Qhuvelia? Why would you go and do a thing like that?"

"I didn't do it on purpose, Calla. By the time Kazamir and I had met a couple of years ago, it had already been done."

"Did your mum promise Qhuvelia her firstborn or something? I thought only the ritual could make someone sell their soul to Qhuvelia."

"Now that you mention it, Calla, perhaps my mum *did* promise me to Qhuvelia and forgot."

"We should go talk to your mum about it right away."

"I agree, Calla."

"Can I ask you something, Catalina?"

Catalina nods.

"Why do you hate me so much? Is it because I replaced you as Katherine's best friend?"

"Yeah."

"You *are* allowed to have more than one best friend, Catalina."

"I know. I just got super jealous of you. You're a *lady*, Calla. I'm just a plain old girl."

"Everyone is special, Catalina, royal or not."

"You really believe so?"

"I do. Come on, let's go talk to your mum."

Calla, now feeling less dizzy, gets up and offers a hand to help Catalina up.

The two new friends, with Faith trotting beside her handler, walk to Headmistress West's office.

Catalina lightly knocks on the door.

"Come in."

Catalina opens the door, beckoning Calla to follow her.

"Catalina? Calla? What are you both doing here? Did you get into another argument?"

"No, ma'am. We're here to ask you some questions." Calla says as both she and Catalina sit down in chairs in front of the head-mistress' desk.

"Oh? Ask away."

"Mum, forgive me for asking this, but did you promise anyone your firstborn's soul? Qhuvelia, perhaps?"

"No, Catalina, I did not."

"Are you 100% sure, ma'am? There's a chance that you could have done so, and had your memory wiped of the incident." Calla tells her headmistress and half-aunt.

"In that case, Calla, I suppose I *could* have done just that. But why would I sell my firstborn's soul to Qhuvelia in the first place, and not my own?"

"Because only a grandchild of mine can have their soul belong to Qhuvelia." Kazamir says, appearing from the shadows.

"How did you get in here? How did you get past the protection spell?" Headmistress West asks.

"You really ought to know that any spell can be reversed, Ella-Rose." Asmi scolds as they appear from the shadows as well.

"What do you want?" Headmistress West asks, stepping in front of her desk and putting the two girls (and Faith) behind her.

"What we've always wanted: to rule the world as King and Sovereign, father and child. Together. Mya?"

Mya comes up behind Headmistress West and the two girls and knocks them all out cold. While Calla loses consciousness, she sees Faith being taken away from her.

~.~

When the three wake up, they smell duct tape and feel it on their mouths, along with ropes around their wrists and ankles.

Calla, leaning on Catalina, does everything in her power to reach for the dagger in her back pocket. Usually, weapons are not permitted at the school, but Calla keeps it with her for protection. Calla gets to work cutting the ropes from her wrists and, after her hands are free, she cuts the rope that's tied around her ankles. She then slowly and carefully takes the duct tape off of her mouth.

After she's freed from her bonds, Calla moves quietly but swiftly to remove the ropes from the wrists and ankles of Catalina and Headmistress West.

Once they're all free, they look at each other in shock before trying to come up with a plan to get out of the office.

Calla, being the only one among them that has magic, is sent out first so her magic can be used on both Kazamir and Asmi.

Calla opens the door just a tad and sees that the coast is surprisingly clear.

Calla leaves the office and silently beckons her fellow hostages forward. Once they reach the end of the corridor, she looks around the corner to see Asmi and Kazamir with their backs turned to them, talking with one another.

"Asmi?" Kazamir suddenly asks. Calla and her companions hide behind the corner of the wall of the corridor.

"What is it, Kazamir?"

"We're being watched. Cause a diversion so I can get away."

"Gladly."

"You know, Kazamir, we can hear your plans for Asmi to cause a diversion so you can get away. Not very smart of you, if you ask me."

"After them, you fool!" Kazamir bellows as Calla, Catalina and Headmistress West all start to run through the school. Asmi is on their tail, a bit faster than Headmistress West, who they catch and knock to the ground.

"Mum!"

"Catalina, Calla, both of you get out of here!"

"We're not leaving anyone behind, Headmistress!" Calla says as she and Catalina help Headmistress West to her feet and the three of them run as they possibly can to somewhere, anywhere, where they'll be safe.

They barely make it to the dining hall, where everyone is eating lunch.

"Everyone, get to safety." Headmistress West commands.

"Kill them all if you must, Asmi!" Kazamir shouts.

Asmi shoots beams of lethal magic out of their hands and the students and faculty barely dodge out of the way in time.

The spell casters of the school gather together and collectively use "Lightning Basalt" on Asmi, who barely makes it past the bolt of lightning.

Kazamir comes forward.

"Miss Calla Lilly, Miss Catalina, join us. You can help us rule the world as father, child and granddaughters." Kazamir says.

"Never, Kazamir. We'll never join you."

"Suit yourself. Mya? Apprehend these unbelievers."

"Right away, Kazamir."

Mya moves to grab Calla and Catalina before Calla shoves Catalina behind her.

"Calla, what are you doing?" Catalina asks.

"If you want us to rule with you, let everyone else go."

"Calla, are you crazy? This is not a good plan!" Catalina asks in a whisper.

"Just roll with it, Catalina." Calla whispers back to her cousin.

"Kazamir, it's *us* you want, right? Let everyone else go, and Catalina and I will willingly go with you to Qhuvelia."

"Speak for yourself." Catalina mutters.

"You'd willingly follow us to the goddess of the underworld?" Asmi asks.

"As if Calla has given us any other choice." Catalina says to herself.

"We will, Asmi. Just let everyone else go, and we will rule by your side, like you said, as father, child and granddaughters."

"Good. Very good. Fine. We agree to your terms. But, Calla, there's something you ought to know."

"What is it, Asmi?" Calla asks, going into a fighting stance to prepare herself to battle her enemies.

"I forced you to use that spell to bring your dear old mummy back to life, forcing Hazel to sacrifice herself."

"You did *what?*" Calla asks.

"You heard me correctly, Calla Lilly Morrison. *I* was the cause of Hazel's death. Well, through *you,* at least. But let me also tell you this: your trauma may have indirectly been caused by me, but you still have trauma, and PTSD. So no need to stop going to therapy or your psychiatrist."

"You betrayed us. You betrayed *me.*"

"And, your point is?"

"How could you?"

"Because I want what I've always wanted and what you have as a royal: power. Something I can grab onto and take for my own use. Well, *our* own use, Kazamir."

"So, what are you going to do to me and Catalina?"

"Nothing. We're simply going to let you follow us to the meeting place where you can pledge your alliance to Qhuvelia."

"And if we don't want to be in Qhuvelia's army?"

"We'll simply kill you where you stand." Kazamir says, stepping forward.

Once Catalina and Calla step forward towards Kazamir and Asmi to try their best to fight, Asmi surrounds the two girls in smoke, and the four of them disappear without a trace.

Screams and shouts of allegiance to Qhuvelia are heard as Calla and Catalina arrive at the meeting place with Asmi and Kazamir.

They've just arrived at the border between the underworld and the living world.

| 12 |

Dad to the Rescue!

It's dark, and there's black and purple mist coming from all sorts of caverns and caves and pillars of rock. As Calla and Catalina's eyes adjust to the dark, as Kazamir and Asmi's are already used to the darkness of the border, the two girls take in their surroundings.

"To cross this border, you must have already sold your soul to Qhuvelia. So, ladies, simply step forward to meet with the goddess of the underworld, and we'll – "

An explosion is suddenly heard from behind Calla, Catalina, Kazamir and Asmi.

The royal guard, with its battalion, has arrived, ready to save both Calla and Catalina, and to arrest Kazamir and Asmi.

"Girls! Come here!"

"You fool! Those girls' souls already belong to Qhuvelia! There's nothing you can do about that, and they can't, either!"

"Not if we have any say in the matter!" Emmitt says, arriving with his fellow archers, including his wife.

"You're right on target, Emmitt." Isabella whispers to her husband.

"You're forgetting both Asmi and I have eyes and ears everywhere, m'lady. Besides, you're too late. The girls were about to pledge their loyalty to Qhuvelia."

"They *what*?"

"Oh, don't be too cross with them, Your Ladyship. They may be 17 years of age, but that doesn't mean they automatically know better than to cross us and Qhuvelia."

"Kazamir!"

The group turns towards the voice.

"Ah, right on time, m'lady. I've just procured both Catalina and Calla Lilly for your army." Kazamir says, putting his arms around the girls before pushing them forward towards the border, where Qhuvelia has her hand stretched out towards the girls.

"Very good, Kazamir. And very good job deceiving Calla, Asmi. You both did excellent jobs obtaining these two fine young ladies for my army."

"We are at your service, my lady. And now, so are these girls." Asmi says, doing their bow-curtsy combination.

"No, they're not!" Emmitt says, aiming an arrow at where he last heard Qhuvelia's voice.

Emmitt looses the arrow and it hits Qhuvelia in her left shoulder. She screams in agony as she falls backward. Asmi and Kazamir immediately go to her to tend to her wound after removing the arrow. Asmi and Kazamir leaving prompts Calla and Catalina to run toward Emmitt and the royal guard.

They escape while Asmi's and Kazamir's backs are turned. Once they're out of the woods – literally *and* figuratively – and are back on school grounds, Calla and Catalina hug each other for the very first time. The majority of the royal guard is with Asmi and Kazamir, ready to arrest them, considering they can't arrest Qhuvelia, since being a goddess prevents them from doing so.

"Do you ladies want to explain why you were going to pledge your alliance to the goddess of the underworld?" Isabella asks.

"We wanted to keep everyone safe. That's the only reason we would have done it."

"We praise your loyalty, your bravery, and your humility. But that still doesn't excuse the fact that you were willing to be so flippant with your loyalty."

"We understand, ma'am." Catalina says.

"Good. The royal guards should be arresting Asmi and Kazamir as we speak."

"Calla, where's Faith?" Catalina asks her new friend.

"I'm not sure. Faith! Faith, here, girl!" Calla calls out. Everyone hears the pitter patter of feet on the ground as Faith runs toward her owner, nearly knocking Calla to the ground. Faith licks Calla's face as the handler and service dog reunite.

"Calla?" Catalina asks as Calla tries to gently push Faith off of herself.

"Yes, Catalina?"

"I'm so sorry for how I've been treating you. I was just jealous that you replaced me as Katherine's best friend and almost girlfriend. Can we start over?"

"Wait, did you say *almost girlfriend*? You mean, I caused the two of you to not be romantic towards one another?"

"Yes, you did. But I'm willing to let that be in the past, if you are, Calla."

"I am."

"I'm glad you two are friends now, Calla."

"Dad!"

"Calla!"

Calla and Kit run into each other's arms and hug for the first time in a while.

"I'm so glad to see you smile again Calla. Smiles look good on you."

"Has anyone seen Katie?" Catalina asks.

"Calla! Catalina!"

"Katherine!"

Catalina and Calla turn to see Katherine running towards them.

When the three girls embrace, a new understanding is said silently between them: they'll never let jealousy tear them apart again.

~.~

Once Kazamir and Asmi have both been caught and sent to the Hartreusian royal dungeon, the students and faculty of the School of the Seven Deities celebrate Emmitt and the royal guard helping save them.

Headmistress West approaches her daughter and her daughter's two new friends.

"I'm so happy you have made friends with Calla, Catalina. I'm guessing you two have forgiven each other for the trouble you've caused each other in the past?"

"Yes, ma'am." Catalina and Calla tell their headmistress.

"Good, because graduation is in a few hours for you twelfth years. So, all twelfth years, please leave to go get ready for graduation. Your parents, guardians and family members will be here before the graduation ceremony."

Catalina, Calla, and Katherine, now all friends, go get ready for graduation with their friends. They try on dresses to wear under their graduation gowns, and do each other's makeup and hair.

"I must say, cousin, you're looking absolutely beautiful." Catalina tells her cousin and friend.

"Why, thank you, my cousin. Katie, you look ravishing as well!" Calla tells her girlfriend.

"Thank you, Calla. To think we're about to graduate and go off into the world! Calla, what will *you* do after we graduate?"

"Well, I'll be in training to possibly take over my stepfather's title, should my Aunt Kessia or cousins Giana and Harris not want the title."

"And if they do?"

"A Likely Story is in need of a new cashier, since Carceia is about to retire. She told me I could have the job if I wanted it, considering that's where my mum and Grandma Hazel used to take me when I was little. Catalina, what are you going to do after we graduate?"

"I was thinking I would see the world before seeking a higher education. I want to become headmistress of this school. It would suit me."

"It really would, Catalina."

"Thank you. Katie, what about you?"

"Well, I'm thinking I'll woo and marry a rich heiress from Rosiary."

"Oh?" Catalina and Calla ask.

"I'm talking about *you*, Calla!"

"Oh. Oh!"

"Oh, just kiss, you two." Catalina says teasingly.

"And ruin our makeup? Absolutely not!"

The three friends laugh with each other, ready for this next milestone in life.

~.~

Headmistress West stands at the front of the twelfth years in the dining hall, where graduation is taking place.

"We are gathered here today to witness the next milestone in these young people's lives. Some may travel the world, others may seek a higher education, while others will go in search of their true purpose in life. Whatever they may do in this next milestone of life, may they do it with love and kindness. Graduates, please come up when your name is called to receive your certificate of completion at the School of the Seven Deities."

Soon, everyone has been called...all, that is, but one: Catalina.

"Catalina Julie West."

Catalina walks up to the front of the hall and she receives her certificate from Headmistress West.

"I'm very proud of you, Catalina, and of how far you've come."

"Thank you, Mum."

Once Catalina takes her seat, Headmistress West asks the graduates to rise.

"I am proud to present the graduating class of 3014."

Everyone claps and cheers for the graduates.

Once the graduating class files out one by one, the other students, faculty members and family members follow them outside for the graduates' picnic.

Groups from all over Gnypso chat and eat their food.

Catalina and Headmistress West sit with Calla and her family, and Katherine and her two dads. Katherine's dog Gizmo, and Calla's dog Faith play with each other around the school grounds, but Faith knows not to stray too far from her owner and handler.

The picnic lasts for hours, and, once it ends, the graduates and their families say goodbye to one another, promising to visit as often as possible.

| 13 |

One Step After Another

The graduates and their families soon leave the school, elated, but also a little sad to leave their past behind there.

Calla, Katherine and one of Katherine's dads Alex ride in one carriage while Burton, Kit's girlfriend Inge and Kit ride in another so they can ride together back to Katherine's home of Demonglen in Lavenderia, which is on the way to Rosiary.

Once Katherine and Calla say goodbye to one another once they reach Lavenderia, Calla and her stepdad and Inge head home.

"I can't believe I'm a graduate of the School of the Seven Deities!" Calla says as she, Inge and Kit head into their estate in Rosiary.

"I can't believe it, either, Calla. So, what's next for you?"

"Well, considering neither Harris, Giana or Aunt Kessia want to become lord or lady of Eburnean, I guess *I'll* be next in line for the title?"

"If you want it, Calla. But, remember, it's a lot of responsibility. Not as much as Aunt Luana and Aunt Nona have, but it's still a lot of work to be a lady of Eburnean. Here's what I'm thinking: you'll move to Eburnean to study under Grandpa, Grandma, Aunt Rose and Uncle Edison this summer, and, by the end of it, you'll make the decision of whether you want the title, or if you want someone else in the family to have it."

"That sounds like a fair idea, Dad."

"Great. You'll have a week to prepare for your journey. It's a long way to Eburnean, considering it's past Lavenderia *and* Hartreusia."

"I won't let you down, Dad."

"I don't doubt you will, Calla. I'm very proud of how far you've come in the last several years."

"Thanks, Dad. It means a lot to me."

"You're welcome. Will you and Faith be down for dinner, or will you both be too excited to eat?"

"I think we'll both be down for dinner."

"That's great to hear. See you then."

"See you later, Dad. Come on, Faith." Faith obediently follows her handler as the two go upstairs to Calla's room to start packing.

Once Calla and Faith enter the room, they're surprised to see the ghost of Calla's great-grandmother Hazel.

"Gr-Grandma Hazel? Is that you?"

"It's me, child. I've been watching over you these past few years."

"You – you have been?"

"Yes. And I'm so sorry that you have developed PTSD. And I'm also sorry to hear your soul no longer belongs to Aileen, but to Qhuvelia."

"You heard about that? Does anyone else know about that?"

"Everyone in the Broken Realm knows about how you were forced to sell your soul to the goddess of the underworld, Calla."

"Oh. So, how do I get back in the allmother's good graces?"

"It's a long and arduous process. It could take days, weeks, months or even years."

"Years?!"

"I'm afraid so, Calla. But don't fret too much about it. What happened to you was not your fault. The only people that are to blame are Asmi and Kazamir. The only thing left now is to act."

"Why did Asmi defect to being a bad person?"

"I don't know. Why are you asking me?"

"I thought you'd know, considering you're watching over us."

"I may be watching over you, but that doesn't make me all-knowing, child."

"Oh. I miss you, Grandma Hazel."

"I miss you, too, Calla. Try not to be so self-destructive. You'll only hurt the people you love that are still alive on Gnypso."

"Is there anything else you want to tell me?"

"I love you, Calla. Never forget that. And I'll be here to greet you in the Broken Realm when the time comes. Aileen told me herself that both I and your mother will be here to welcome you."

"I love you, too, Grandma Hazel. And I'm sorry."

"Don't be sorry, Calla. You were young and naïve back then. There's nothing that could have been done to save me. I'd better go."

"Grandma Hazel?"

"Yes, child?"

"How long were you alive?"

"More than a millennium."

"So, you were there when the world ended?"

"I was there then, and even before that. I was there during the first and second world wars on Earth."

"I've heard about those. They were terrible conflicts."

"That's putting it mildly, Calla. I must get going, child. If you need me, I will always be with you. Remember, dear, I'll always love you."

"And I'll always love you, Grandma Hazel."

Hazel's spirit fades away and Faith and Calla are left alone. Calla soon starts packing for her journey to Eburnean.

A week later, Calla and Faith board Kit's royal carriage bound for Dimborn in Eburnean, about a mile from Calla's old school.

Once goodbyes are exchanged between Kit, Inge and Calla, the carriage leaves the Morrison estate.

Calla and her service dog Faith soon reach Eburnean. Eburnean is a small country, and has only one village, but two castles, one for the Morrison family, the other for the School of the Seven Deities.

After Calla and Faith reach the manor in Eburnean, her grandma, grandpa, aunt, great-aunt, great-uncle and first cousins once removed are there to greet her.

"Calla, darling! Welcome to the Morrison manor in Eburnean. I trust you had a pleasant journey?"

"I did, Lady Rose."

The two start walking towards the manor as the servants carry Calla's and Faith's things into the manor towards her guest suite.

"Your stepfather told us about your PTSD. Just know that we will do everything we can to make sure you are as comfortable as possible."

"Thank you, Lady Rose."

"You're welcome. A feast has been prepared in your honor, and we will start training to become Lady of Eburnean the day after to-morrow, because I want you to spend some quality time with your relatives that live here."

"Thank you kindly, Lady Rose. It's an honor to be taught by someone such as yourself."

"The pleasure's all mine, dear. Now, go upstairs and get settled. A servant will come round to let you know dinner is ready."

Calla nods and curtsies to her great-aunt and other relatives before she and Faith head upstairs to unpack and rest a bit from their long journey from Rosiary.

Calla uses her phone to play a bit of pop music to listen to while she unpacks her and Faith's belongings. Calla dances and sings along while unpacking, and, soon, she is finished unpacking her belongings that will last the next three months.

Calla goes over to her bookcase, where she's unpacked and organized her books, and she selects a book to read while she waits for a servant to come and fetch her for dinner.

After Calla reads for a while, there's a knock on the door of her guest suite.

"Lady Calla? This is Vanessa, one of the servants. It's time for dinner."

"Thank you, Vanessa. I'll be down in a minute."

"Alright, ma'am."

Calla reluctantly puts her book away and gets dressed in one of her finest gowns – a gown inspired by the one her mother wore at her ladyship ceremony, a purple dress with a gold trim. She wants to wear this gown as often as possible, and plans to wear it when Calla herself becomes a lady of Eburnean.

Calla and Faith head down to dinner and Calla takes her seat while Faith goes under Calla's chair as usual.

A dinner of Hazel's summer stew is served, and Calla tries her best to enjoy it, despite the pain it causes her to eat something that was made by someone so beloved.

Two days later, Calla and her Great-Aunt Rose make their way to the ballroom so Rose can teach everything she knows to Calla to prepare her for her ladyship ceremony and the grand ball that will follow after.

It's a long and arduous process for both Rose and Calla, teaching this new graduate from the School of the Seven Deities and being taught everything Calla needs to know about becoming and being a lady.

Calla learns proper social skills and etiquette, how to stand, sit, dance, eat, drink and even be merry.

By the time Calla has perfected her waltz, it's nearly sunrise, and both Calla and her great-aunt are exhausted.

"Off to bed, Calla. There's much more to teach you later today."

Calla tiredly curtsies to her great-aunt, then heads off to bed, Faith following closely behind her handler.

Later that day, when Calla has had a break from activities around the manor, she heads to a secluded part of the library with her tablet and earphones to videocall Kit.

"How's my Calla Lilly doing?"

"I'm doing fine, Dad. Just exhausted."

"Aunt Kessia and Grandma and Grandpa aren't working you too hard, are they?"

"It's not them. It's Great-Aunt Rose."

"Oh?"

"She's driving me mad! Teaching me all these things on how to become a proper lady even when I don't even know if I want to become one!"

"You signed up for this, Calla. Remember that."

"I know, Dad. I'm just so tired."

"Try to carve out some time for leisure and rest. Things will get easier, Calla. Just remember: you've – "

"'You've gotten through all of your worst days thus far.' I know, Dad."

"That's my girl. Now, head off to your room to take a nap."

"I will, Dad."

"Good girl. Love you, kiddo."

"Love you, too, Dad."

Calla hangs up the videocall and leaves the room where she was talking to Kit. She bumps into her cousin Giana.

"Giana! Hey! What – what are you up to?"

"Oh, not much, Calla. Just looking around for a book to read."

"In one of the study rooms?"

"I heard you talking to Kit."

"Oh?"

"And I heard you complaining that my mum is driving you mad."

"Oh."

"Who gave you the right to say such a thing?"

"Well, who gave you the right to eavesdrop on my private conversation?"

Giana crosses her arms.

"Touché. Shall we just forget this conversation ever occurred?"

"Fine by me, Giana. Now, if you'll excuse me, I'm going to take a nap before dinner."

"Calla, wait."

"What?"

"Is it true that you sold your soul to Qhuvelia?"

"It was unwillingly, but, yes, I did."

"How are you going to get back in Aileen's good graces?"

"I don't know. Any ideas?"

"You could make a sacrifice – an offering of sorts."

"That's certainly an idea. Any suggestions, Giana?"

"We could always sacrifice Harris."

"But he's your brother!"

"And?"

"I would never sacrifice someone you're so close to. Yes, he's a pain, but he's still family."

"I guess you're right, Calla. Walk with me to the garden?"

"Of course, Giana."

Giana and Calla take a stroll arm-in-arm around the back garden, looking at and smelling the roses.

"I must say, I am quite impressed with the progress you've made since you've arrived."

"I think your mother is trying to kill me, Giana."

"Oh, nonsense. Mum is trying her best to make sure you turn into a proper lady."

"I thought that's what the School of the Seven Deities was for."

"That school is for teaching good manners and etiquette, not for training royals."

"I guess that makes sense."

"I'm glad you see it that way. Let me see...I guess I could teach you how to waltz properly."

"My waltzing is fine, Giana."

"'Fine' may not cut it at your ball. However will you impress future suitors?"

"F-future *what?*"

"Future suitors! You *are* single, are you not?"

"I am not. I'm dating Katherine Griffiths, and I'm sure she's the love of my life."

"Hmm."

"'Hmm' what?"

"Just the fact that you're dating a commoner."

"So? Queen Consort Nona was once a commoner herself, and look at her now. She's half of the monarchy!"

"Oh, pish posh. Katherine Griffiths knows nothing about being a proper lady."

"Are you suggesting that I break up with my girlfriend of five years?"

"I'm not just suggesting it, I'm also commanding it."

"Giana, you may be older than me, but you are *not* the boss of me."

"Then why do you do what I say?"

"What – what are you talking about?"

"I'm talking about our walk in the garden. You could have said 'no', but you didn't. Why?"

"B-because I needed the fresh air."

"Alright. If you say so."

"I *do* say so!"

Giana and Calla continue walking around the garden when they spot Harris practicing his fencing with his fencing partner, Kieran. Kieran takes off his fencing helmet and his hair blows in the wind like in an old cartoon. Calla's mouth gapes open.

"Well, don't let the flies in, or let him see you, Calla." Giana whispers. Giana leads her cousin away from the two young men.

"And don't even think about it."

"Why not?"

"Because, he's Harris's boyfriend...in fact, I suspect Harris will be proposing to Kieran any day now."

"So, he's gay."

"No, he's bisexual. There's a difference, Calla."

"I know very well that there's a difference, Giana. Besides, I shouldn't even be looking at Kieran."

"Why? Because of your girlfriend?"

"Yes! And for another thing, I'm not bisexual or pansexual or anything like that! I'm a lesbian!"

"Shhh...don't let the others hear you."

"Why not? 'Lesbian' is not a dirty word, as the Ancients would have said."

"Who cares about the Ancients? They're dead, and long dead at that."

"They may be long gone, but I know one person who walked among them."

"Who?"

"My Grandma Hazel. Well, I guess she was *everyone's* Grandma Hazel. She was special like that." Calla suddenly looks downcast.

"What is it, Calla?"

"She *was* special, Giana. And she's gone because of me. No matter what Asmi says, even if they somehow controlled me to make Hazel sacrifice herself, it was my fault for looking up the spell in the first place."

"Don't go blaming yourself, even though you should have known better."

"That's my point! I *should* have known better, but I didn't. What is wrong with me?" Calla sinks to the ground in her gown, mud covering the hems of her skirts.

"Calla Lilly, I am surprised at you!"

"What do you mean?"

"What I mean is, yes, you should have known better and read the fine print about the spell you used, but you need to forgive yourself for your past mistakes, and let go of them as well."

"How?"

"With time, and with confidence. You *can* and you *will* be able to forgive yourself and let go of your past mistakes, Calla. I believe in you."

"You do?"

"I do."

"I thought you hated me for insulting your mother."

"I've said worse things to her face, and didn't get out of the room without a talking to. You'll get through this training, Calla. Unless you don't want the position after all." Giana says, raising her eyebrow.

Calla nods, and gets up.

"I *do* want this position. I *do* want to become high lady of Eburnean, and I *will* do everything in my power to make sure I get it. Come on, Giana. Let's go train to become proper ladies."

"Oh, you go on ahead."

"You're not coming with me?"

"I'm already lady of Eburnean, and there are different customs and traditions and such that I've been learning about since I could form a coherent thought! You go, and I'll stay behind."

"Alright. I'll see you at dinner, then?"

"You sure will."

Once Calla leaves the area, Giana wanders towards the woods of South Eburnean.

"Miss Giana. How lovely to see you."

"Who is it? Who's there?" Giana asks, looking towards the voice.

"I am Asmi, a child of your greatest enemy: Kazamir Riker."

"I've never even *met* Kazamir, Asmi. And aren't you supposed to be in prison?"

"I am. Well, I *was*, but I escaped. Kazamir will surely be put to death for helping me escape. But c'est la vie."

"Why are you here? And why am I even *talking* to you? I should be going and getting the royal guard so they can arrest you and hold you here until the Hartreusian royal guards arrive."

"Or we could make a deal."

"I would never make a deal with someone like you."

"Oh? And why not?"

"Because you hurt my cousin Calla."

"Oh, that girl? She's got more power flowing in her veins than she realizes. When she sold her soul to Qhuvelia, dark magic began going into her bloodstream. Soon, she'll become a darker version of herself, and there's nothing anyone can do to stop it. Not even Hazel, may she rest in peace, could stop it. The old bat couldn't save herself from spilling the secret about Celeste's true maternal heritage, nor could she save herself from the sacrifice Calla forced her to make."

"But Calla said that *you* forced her to make Hazel sacrifice herself."

"I was lying. I'm a good actor, aren't I? I should really try out for the theater every now and again. If I weren't a wanted criminal, that is."

"So...Calla really *was* the cause of Hazel's death. She should be the one in prison. I can't have a criminal running a country such as Eburnean! Therefore, I shall report my findings to my mother, and have Calla arrested. Thank you for this development. Um, should my mother ask how I came to know this information, how can I explain that to her?"

"You simply tell her an outside force told you the real truth, and that Calla should be arrested as soon as possible. This isn't the first time Calla Lilly has gotten in trouble with the law, and I can guarantee it won't be the last. Go, Giana. Go tell the world this truth."

Giana nods, turns away and then remembers she'd have to thank Asmi for this information. But when she turns back to face them, Asmi has already slipped away.

Giana heads back to the manor, and finds her mother in the ballroom, helping Calla practice her waltz.

"Stop the music. Giana! Where have you been?"

"Where I've been isn't that important, Mother. But what *is* important is the information I bring."

"Oh?"

"Calla Lilly Morrison...she *was* the cause of Hazel's death. It wasn't an outside force, but Calla herself, and her alone."

"And how did you come to know about this information?"

"I got this information from an outside source, Mum. They told me the real truth. We must arrest Calla as soon as possible!"

"Not until a trial has been held."

"For what reason, Mother? We all know Calla is guilty. Even she herself knows it!"

Calla steps up to Giana and Rose.

"It's true, Great-Aunt Rose. I *am* guilty about and the cause of Hazel's death. It would be best for me to be arrested without a trial and be sentenced to death. An eye for an eye, as the Ancients used to say."

"An eye for an eye, child, and the whole world goes blind." Rose tells her grand-niece.

"Please, Aunt Rose, I *must* be punished for my crime."

"You actually *want* to be stripped of your title and your dignity?"

"Can't lose what I no longer have."

Rose sighs.

"The most I can do, Calla, is send you home."

It is then Calla's turn to sigh.

"Very well. I suppose that that *is* the most you can do."

"I'm glad we agree. Go and pack your things, and I shall send word to your stepfather that you will be making an early trip home."

~.~

"And, pardon me for saying this, Aunt Rose, but are you sure Giana was telling the absolute and honest-to-Aileen truth?"

"My daughter has never been known to lie, Kit. And neither has Calla. Do you suppose that, perhaps, Giana has been misled to believe something?"

"I'm not sure, Aunt Rose. I believe that I should take this to the queens, and see if they believe that Giana was misled, or if – if my stepdaughter really is the cause of Hazel's death."

"I'm so sorry it's come to this, Kit. I wish I had the power to change it all for the better, but I'm afraid even I don't have that power."

"I understand, Aunt Rose, and thank you."

| 14 |

Calla's Trial

Once Calla has reached her home in Rosiary, she and Faith leave the carriage. Kit and Inge are both there, looking worried for Calla.

"Did you have a safe trip home, Calla?" Kit asks, hugging his stepdaughter.

"I did, Dad. But, right now, I'm so tired, I can barely stand."

"Go inside and get some rest. We'll talk about things in the morning."

"Alright." Calla looks rather disappointed that she won't be punished straight away, as she wants to get her talking to over with and her punishment started as soon as possible. But the poor girl can barely keep her eyes open, let alone pay attention to the stern talking to she'll receive from her family members.

Faith and Calla head upstairs to her room, and, after getting ready for bed, Calla and Faith drift off to sleep.

In the middle of the night, Calla wakes up and sees a figure glowing at the foot of her bed. As Calla's eyes adjust to the dark, she sees that it's her Great-Grandma Hazel.

"G-Grandma Hazel?"

"I'm here, child. But I can only stay for a moment."

"What is it, Grandma Hazel? I'm awfully tired from my journey."

"I know you are, Calla. But what I have to say is important: don't let your guilt get the best of you."

"What does that mean?"

"It means that you must not let Asmi or Kazamir or Qhuvelia win."

"What do they have to do with any of this?"

"They have everything to do with this, Calla. Asmi started working for Qhuvelia when you were just a baby. They've been working together with Kazamir to make sure that your soul belongs only to Qhuvelia."

Hazel's spirit starts fading away.

"Grandma Hazel, don't go!"

"I'm afraid I don't have a choice. I'll see you in the next life, many, many, *many* years from now. Now go back to sleep, Calla."

Calla bolts up in bed, thinking it was all a dream. But the note by her bed says otherwise.

"Don't blame yourself for my death, Calla. It was all Asmi's and Kazamir's doings. Love, Grandma Hazel."

Calla grabs the note and heads downstairs to talk to her stepdad about it, with Faith following closely behind.

"Dad...I have to tell you something."

"What is it, Calla? Are you alright?"

"I'm fine, Dad. It's just that Grandma Hazel visited me last night and she told me that I shouldn't let my guilt get the best of me, and that I'm not to blame for her death." Calla continues telling her stepdad the story of what Hazel had told her the night before.

"Are you sure you weren't just dreaming, Calla?"

"I'm sure. Remember when Mum came during our camping trip?"

"I do. I get what you're saying now, Calla. Thank you for telling me. Now, about your upcoming trial: I will do everything in my power to make sure you're not found guilty. We all know it wasn't your fault directly."

"I know that. But how can I tell the court that I was being mind-controlled to look up the spell to bring Mum back and Grandma Hazel ended up sacrificing herself so Mum wouldn't be in any pain?" Calla says, all in a rush while pacing back and forth around the casual dining hall.

"You just tell the truth, and if they don't believe you, I know the lawyer I hired for you will do everything in her power to make sure that you come out of the courtroom innocent and unscathed."

"Thank you, Dad."

"You're welcome. Would you like to eat something for breakfast, or are your nerves getting the best of you?"

"I don't think I could eat right now. Maybe after the trial is over?"

"The trial may take more than one day, sweetheart. At least *try* to eat something between the trial days?"

"I'll try my best, Dad. That's all I can say for right now."

"That's good enough for me."

That afternoon, Calla's trial takes place in a local courthouse in Bellamy in Rosiary.

"Lady Calla, is it true that you are on trial for murdering your own great-grandmother?"

"Yes, that is accurate."

"And is it true that you deliberately murdered Hazel?"

"No, of course not!"

"Please tell the court exactly what happened that day."

"Well, my girlfriend Katherine and I made a fort in my room, and we were talking about how much I missed my mum." Calla continues telling her side of the story, and, soon, because of her moving story, there's not a dry eye in the courtroom.

Katherine is soon called up to the witness stand to tell her perspective of that day that Hazel met her untimely death. She does, and her story, obviously, matches up with what Calla had told the court. By the time Katherine has finished telling her story, it's late into the evening, and court is adjourned for the night.

Katherine and Calla hug each other, hopeful that the court will rule in Calla's favor, and that Asmi and Kazamir will eventually be brought to justice. The father and child will tell their sides of the story the next day through a videocall.

That night comes and goes, and Asmi and Kazamir are video-called during the trial to tell their perceptions of the story.

"Mr. Riker, is it true that you and your associate Asmi were told by Qhuvelia herself, the goddess of the underworld, that Calla would have to sell her soul to Qhuvelia to make sure that Calla did not get into any more trouble of her own volition?"

The court begins to murmur at this new information.

"Yes, that is correct."

"And are you aware that you had helped sell a minor's soul to Qhuvelia?"

"I didn't know – I wasn't aware that there was an age limit on whose soul belongs to Qhuvelia."

"It's in all the old stories about the gods and goddesses of Destiny."

"But Qhuvelia is not one of those. Or am I wrong in that?"

"No, you are not wrong in that, Kazamir. It is true that Qhuvelia's religion, Autonomism, is separate from that of the religion of Destinism."

"That's what I thought. Is there a reason we're talking about this?"

"I'll ask the questions here, Mr. Riker. Calla was about 17 when she unwillingly sold her soul to Qhuvelia, is that correct?"

"Yes." Kazamir sneers.

"In addition, was that with or without the knowledge that children – even if they're almost adults – are unable to give up their soul to anyone unless they have their own free will?"

Kazamir begins to sputter.

"Definitely without. Wait, does that mean that – ?"

"Yes. That means that neither Calla Lilly Morrison, nor her cousin, Catalina West, have had their soul sold to Qhuvelia, and have belonged to Aileen since they day they were dedicated to her."

"But does that mean that Calla actually did have free will when it came to Hazel's death?"

"I'm afraid I can't answer that, Mr. Riker. Only Asmi can answer that pertinent question. Mr. Riker may step down."

Soon, Asmi takes the stand as the next person to be interrogated by Calla's lawyer.

"Asmi, is it true that, through your grandmother Hazel, you are able to control others' minds?"

"Yes, it's true. And, to answer your next question, yes, I did force Calla to use that spell to try to get her mum back, thus being the cause of Hazel's death."

"So you, Asmi, are the indirect cause of Hazel's death, by means of mind-controlling Calla Lilly Morrison. Is that accurate?"

"Yes."

"No further questions."

Other witnesses, such as Allison, Calla's old nanny, is called to the witness stand to state her case and tell her perspective.

Soon, all the people that need to testify have spoken, and the jury soon after reaches a verdict.

"On the count of murder in the third degree, how do you, the jury, find Lady Calla Lilly Morrison?"

"We, the jury, find Lady Calla Lilly Morrison not guilty of third degree murder."

"And on two counts of murder in the first degree, how do you, the jury, find Asmi?"

"We, the jury, find Asmi guilty of first degree murder."

"And on the count of child endangerment, how do you, the jury, find Kazamir Riker?"

"We, the jury, find Kazamir Riker guilty of two counts of child endangerment."

"Court is dismissed, and both Kazamir Riker and Asmi will be brought in from Hartreusia for sentencing."

Once Katherine, Calla, Kit and Inge are all out of the courtroom, they all hug each other, glad that it turned out for the better, instead of turning out for the worse.

A few weeks later, Kazamir and Asmi are both sentenced to prison for life, and all seems to be well.

Katherine and Calla are walking out in the garden one day a few months after Kazamir and Asmi are sentenced.

"Katie...*Katherine.* I wanted to ask you something, now that I know that I'm not truly guilty."

"What is it, Calla?"

Calla kneels down on her left knee and takes out a ring she had bought just a month before this day, and she had gotten Katherine's dads' blessings.

"Katherine Griffiths, would you like to spend the rest of your life with me? Will you marry me?"

"Yes, Calla! Yes, I'll marry you! But, first." Katherine then kneels in front of Calla and takes out a ring that *she* had bought just a month before, and she had gotten both Kit's and Emmitt's blessings.

"Calla Lilly Morrison, will you make me the happiest woman alive? Will you marry me?"

"Yes, Katherine! Yes, I'll marry you!"

Calla puts Katherine's engagement ring on Katherine's finger, and Katherine puts Calla's ring on Calla's finger, and the two kiss.

They know that, no matter what they go through, they'll always have each other.

Katherine's dads, Alex and Burton, along with Kit, Inge, Emmitt, and Isabella all come out to congratulate the newly-engaged couple.

And, with Calla and Katherine looking at their families, soon to be joined as one big family, look out at the world, unsure of what will come next for them, but sure that they will be there for each other, no matter what is thrown their way.

| 15 |

Calla Is Kidnapped

A few days after Katherine and Calla's double proposal and engagement, Kit throws a ball in their honor. The two ladies both wear white ensembles that are different from each other, Katherine a suit with pink undertones, as pink is Calla's favorite color. Calla wears a dress that is much like her gown that she was going to wear when she officially became a lady of Eburnean. The title of lord will now go to Harris and his new fiancé, Kieran, who both want the title for themselves and raise a family of their own, to carry on Harris' father's legacy.

The ball, in true Gnypsonian fashion, lasts all night and most of the early morning.

The party starts at around 5pm, and the guests are allowed in at 4:45.

The engagement party starts with Katherine's and Calla's first dance as an engaged couple. The food that is served comes from all areas of Gnypso, and is enjoyed by all in attendance.

There are games, line dances and speeches. Kit and Emmitt both collaborate to embarrass Calla, while Alex and Burton take turns embarrassing their own daughter.

The guests guess who is the better cook, the better dancer, the better singer, etc., and the brides-to-be provide the answers with The Shoe Game, which consists of Calla and Katherine exchanging one of their shoes, and holding one of them up according to the corresponding answer.

Once the ball ends, all those in attendance, including the future Mrs. and Mrs. Morrison, are all tuckered out and ready for bed.

Katherine and Calla head upstairs to bed, with Faith in tow, and get ready for bed. After the two girls have gone to bed, Kit peeks into the room and sees that both girls are fast asleep, and he soon heads to bed himself, happy that his stepdaughter is happy.

That evening, a figure sneaks in undetected to Calla's room, and snatches her from her bed, using poppyseed oil to make sure she doesn't wake up and scream.

When Katherine wakes the next morning, she sees that her fiancée is nowhere to be found.

"Guards! Help! I need help in here!"

"Katherine? What's the matter?"

"It's Calla. She's gone missing."

"We'll find her, Katherine. Have no doubts about that."

"Oh, I do hope Calla is alright, wherever she is."

"We'll make sure she is, Katherine. We promise. Please wait here in the estate."

Once the guards leave to go find Calla, Katherine begins thinking that Calla has gotten kidnapped quite a lot in her life, and she wonders if marrying her really is the best idea.

She heads out to find Kit and talk to him, and she finds him in his study.

"Kit? Could I have a word with you?"

"Of course, Katie. What seems to be the trouble?"

"I'm guessing you didn't hear."

"Hear what?"

"That Calla's missing."

"WHAT?!"

"I can't believe it, either, sir. But that's not why I'm here."

"Whatever it is, unless it's an emergency, can't it wait until Calla is safe and home?"

"I understand, sir. I'll wait to talk with you until Calla is safe at home."

"Thank you for being so considerate, Katie. It means a lot to me. Calla is very lucky to have you." Kit gets up, pats Katherine on her shoulder and leaves the room.

"Yes, but am *I* lucky to have Calla?" Katherine mutters to herself once Kit is out of earshot.

When Katherine heads downstairs, everyone is waiting for her, wondering where Calla is, and if she's alright.

"Lady Katherine, I'm so sorry you had to witness Lady Calla being kidnapped once again."

"Oh, I was actually asleep when she was kidnapped. I believe if I hadn't been asleep, I would have sounded the alarm, so to speak."

The crowd begins to murmur and mutter to one another and to themselves, wondering who had kidnapped Calla.

"But the royal guard will stop at nothing to find her. I just hope they find her soon."

Meanwhile, Calla is on horseback with her captor, and she's starting to wake up.

"Pssst. Hey, kid. Wake up. You can trust me." The captor says before lowering their mask and revealing who they are to Calla, who scoffs when she sees who it is that had kidnapped her.

"Says the traitor to everyone on Gnypso. Why do you want me, Asmi? For revenge? Power?"

"I want to prove my innocence, because, I, too, had my soul sold to Qhuvelia."

"And why should I believe you? You tried to frame me for Hazel's death when it was *really* you who caused her death by mind-controlling me."

"That may be what you think, but, in truth, it was really Qhuvelia's second-in-command who did that."

"And who is Qhuvelia's second-in-command?"

"That I will tell you at another time. Right now, I do believe we're being followed by your royal guard."

"Gee, I wonder why. Oh, wait: you kidnapped a lady of Rosiary!"

"There's no reason you should trust me, but I'm asking, friend to friend, to – "

"We are *not* friends. Not anymore, after what you did to me and my cousin."

"I don't blame you, Calla. But, please, you have to believe that Qhuvelia's second-in-command is to blame for Hazel."

"And you won't tell me who that is because..."

"Because I literally can't. Qhuvelia would have my head, sending me to an early death if I were to spill who her second-in-command is."

"And that would be a bad thing because..."

"Because I haven't found my true love, whoever they may be. I must congratulate you, Calla, on your engagement. Well, for now, at least."

"What are you talking about?"

"I'm talking about the fact that your little fiancée Katherine has been having second thoughts because you keep getting kidnapped, and she doesn't believe being with someone who keeps getting kidnapped is worthwhile."

"I don't believe you."

"And there's no reason that you *should* believe me. But I'm running out of time."

"And what exactly does that mean?"

"It means that the end of the world as we know it is coming, and there's no way to prevent it or prolong it...but there are ways to speed up the process."

"And what are those ways, just so I can know not to do them?"

"You think anyone would tell *me* those things? Simple, naïve Calla Lilly...you still have a lot to learn about the world, and the afterlife."

"Is there anything you *can* tell me about the end of the world?"

"Only that it will happen sooner than you think, but you must listen to me, Calla. When people panic and get scared, they may become violent at times. You must try your hardest to stay away from people who are loose cannons."

"And I should believe you. Just like that. Just like nothing has happened between us. Just like *you* didn't murder Hazel."

"I understand you're upset, Calla."

"How could you? You *murdered* my great-grandmother, which caused practically the whole world to hate me, including my classmates, causing me to develop PTSD and need a service dog. And another thing – "

"Shhh. Do you hear that?"

"You just want me to stop talking."

"Don't speak, Calla. Listen."

Calla closes her mouth and her eyes and listens. She hears a muttering chatter coming from the distance ahead of her and Asmi.

"I've only heard legends about rabid elves."

"Stay here, and don't get bitten. I can handle this."

Asmi dismounts, expecting Calla to stay on the horse, but she leaps down after them, drawing a spare sword from one of Asmi's two sheaths. A look of determination crosses her face, and she glances over at her Auncle Asmi, who is looking on proudly. They nod at Calla and, together, the two rush at the pack of rabid elves, slashing and dicing until the elves are all dead in piles around the field.

"Halt! Stop in the name of the queens!"

"This is where I must leave you, Calla. I bid you farewell, and I hope to see you soon."

"Asmi, what - ?"

In a flash of smoke, Asmi disappears, leaving a very confused and rather dazed Calla behind.

"Lady Calla! Are you alright? Are you hurt?"

"I'm fine...just a little bit dazed, that's all."

"We're here to take you back to the Morrison estate. Where is your captor?"

"They...they disappeared in a flash of smoke. Didn't you see the dead rabid...elves?" Calla asks as she looks around her, seeing that the elves all seemingly disappeared with Asmi.

Qhuvelia suddenly appears out of the ground, and she sucks out Calla's soul. Calla screams as her soul is removed from her body.

That's when Calla bolts awake, breathing heavy and sweating.

She looks around her and sees she's in a forest alone. She pinches herself, and she's not dreaming.

"Where am I?" Calla asks no one.

"Do not fear, my child. I am here to guide you home."

"Grandma Hazel?"

"I am only known as Hazel to a lot of you, well, all of you, actually, but, where I come from, I am known by a different name." Hazel transforms from an old lady into someone who looks timeless.

| 16 |

Calla Meets Someone Very Special

"That dream you had, little Calla, was not a dream to be taken lightly."

"Who – who are you?"

"Don't you know who I am, from the picture books your dear mother used to read you when you were little?"

"Wait..."

Calla's mind flashes back to when she was two, a memory of her mother, Celeste, reading a book to her about the gods and goddesses of Destiny. At the end, a beautiful goddess with golden hair sticks out to toddler Calla, and current Calla's mind reels with confusion, excitement and then, finally, understanding.

"Aileen? The goddess of all humans and creatures?"

"Yes. I am Aileen, the goddess of all beings, living and dead."

"Your Holiness, where is my great-grandmother Hazel?"

"I was her. She told you that she's been here for more than a millennium, did she not?"

"Y-yes, ma'am."

"That is true. I've been here since the end of the old world, Earth, and the beginning of the new one, Gnypso. I took the form of an old woman so you, and everyone else, would trust me."

"So, you've deceived me, deceived *everyone* for all time?"

"Yes, Calla. I deceived everyone so they would not be afraid of me in my true form."

"I see."

Calla backs up, in awe of Aileen's wonderfulness and brightness.

"There's no need to be afraid, little Calla. Would you prefer me in the form of your great-grandmother Hazel?"

"I-I'm not sure."

"Or someone else you know, perhaps? Maybe...your mother?"

Aileen transforms from her true goddess self into the kind, warm, and loving Celeste Calla remembers.

"N-no. That makes me even more uncomfortable."

"Yes, I thought it might make you so. I apologize for my changing into your loved ones."

"It's – it's alright. You didn't know."

"But I did, Calla. I see all, and I know all, even little thoughts such as the ones you've been having since I showed you my true self."

"Aileen?"

"Yes, my child?"

"You said that you were going to help me get out of here?"

Aileen moves and stands next to Calla, crouching next to her, one hand on her shoulder and the other pointing towards the clearing.

"Yes. Follow the trees. They will guide you out into the clearing, where the royal guard is waiting for you. Asmi had dumped you here earlier, and I decided to have a talk with them."

"Y-you did?"

"Yes. I showed up as Hazel, and I told them off for abandoning a child such as yourself. You may be getting married soon, but you are technically still a child."

"I see."

"You're not still cross about my lies to you, are you, Miss Calla?"

"I'm not really sure."

"I understand if you are."

"You do?"

"Yes. My sister happens to be the goddess of the underworld, and she deceived me once, so I banished her to the underworld and gave her the title you all know today."

"Qhu-Qhuvelia is your sister?"

"She is."

"She's really scary. No offense."

Aileen laughs at this.

"Do not be afraid of offending me, Calla. I've heard every offending sentence and word in the book, including that one."

"Alright."

"And, besides, Qhuvelia is only scary when she needs to be. On the rare occasions when she and I meet, she's actually quite playful. This is where I leave you, Calla. I wish you luck on the rest of your journey back home."

"Aileen?"

"Yes?"

"You said that my dream was not a dream to be taken lightly. Does that mean the end of the world is upon us? And where exactly did my dream begin and end?"

"Asmi did tell you about the end of the world being sooner than you think, and that is true. And your dream began long ago, before you leapt off of the horse, and it ended when you woke up here."

"I think I understand now. Thank you, Aileen."

"You're welcome. Now go, Calla. I'll always be with you. And don't tell anyone."

As Calla walks back to the clearing, she glances back and sees Aileen, changing her waving form from Aileen to Hazel to Celeste, then back to Aileen, all in a flash of glitchy light quicker than a second.

Once Calla reaches the clearing, the royal guard approaches her.

"Lady Calla! We were about to enter the forest when we saw you coming out of it. Are you alright? Are you hurt?"

"I'm alright, Captain. Just take me home, please. I've been through quite the ordeal." Calla says, meaning that in two ways: Asmi kidnapping her and meeting the allmother.

"Right away, m'lady."

Calla mounts the horse behind the captain and they ride off back towards Rosiary.

Once they reach Rosiary about half a day later, Kit, Faith, Emmitt, Isabella, Inge, Katherine, Alex, Burton, Victoria and little Celeste are all there to see that Calla has made it back home safely.

"Calla! Oh, sweetheart! Are you alright?" Kit asks, embracing his stepdaughter.

"I'm fine, Dad. I'd like to have a talk with my fiancée, if that's alright with everyone."

Katherine and Calla walk hand-in-hand to the estate's library, with Alex, Burton, Kit, Inge, Emmitt and Isabella all looking after them worriedly.

Calla and Katherine head into a secluded area of the library where no one will overhear or disturb them.

"Calla, what's all this about?"

"Asmi told me about you having second thoughts about us. That my getting kidnapped is too much for you to handle."

"What? Yes, I was having second thoughts about us. But that doesn't mean they haven't disappeared. I still want to marry you,

Calla Lilly Morrison! And I won't give up on you or us. You getting kidnapped is possibly something that we can prevent together as a team."

"You really think so, Katie?"

"I know so, Calla. I will always be there for you, for better or for worse, through thick and thin. I promise. You matter to me, even if you don't think you do. And I hope I matter to you as well."

"You do. You matter so much to me, Katherine. I promise I won't abandon you. Still love me?"

"Forever and ever and always, my darling. Forever and ever and always."

| 17 |

Wedded Bliss

A few months pass without incident, and soon, the royal wedding of Calla Lilly Morrison and Katherine Griffiths is upon everyone, and everyone is at the Morrison estate, milling about and getting the manor ready for Calla's and Katherine's big day.

Calla, meanwhile, is waiting in her stepfather's office, wearing a dress exactly like the one her mother wore on her and Kit's wedding day: a floor-length white dress with a gold trim, cap sleeves, and lace detailing all over the dress. Kit had helped Calla design her dress, since it's one of the most important days in Calla's life. She'll be wearing a tiara with pink stones and a cathedral veil.

In another part of the estate, in what will be her and Calla's room, Katherine is wearing a white pantsuit with pink undertones, and she's getting antsy, but she is not, under any circumstances, having second thoughts about marrying Calla. The two were a match made in the Broken Realm, and both Calla and Katherine believe that, along with everyone else that knows them, which, after the incident with Hazel, everyone knows about them, even not considering the fact that Calla is royalty.

Katherine peeks out from the bedroom and looks to the left and right and sees only the guards posted outside every door.

Once she closes the door back, she slides down the wall and sighs.

"Katie? Are you alright, princess?" Alex asks his daughter.

"I'm fine, Daddy. I'm just ready to get this show on the road."

"I know, sweetie. Can Dad and I come in?"

"I guess."

Alex and Burton enter the room, where boxes are strewn about with things from Katie's room back home.

"Oh, Katie. You look beautiful. Oh, you almost forgot this." Burton gently places a birdcage veil on Katherine's head.

"Thanks, Dad. I love you guys."

"We love you, too." Alex and Burton hug their daughter and they leave her be to collect her thoughts before the top of the hour, when the wedding will begin.

The top of the hour comes sooner than anyone expects, and Alex and Burton escort their daughter to the front of the wedding chapel in Rosiary. Once Katherine reaches the front of the chapel, she kisses both of her dads on their cheeks, and waits for the entrance of her wife-to-be.

Soon, the doors of the chapel open and Calla enters on the arms of her two dads: Kit, her stepfather, and Emmitt, her biological father.

Calla soon joins hands with her wife-to-be, and personal vows begin and rings are exchanged, and, soon Calla and Katherine are pronounced wives, pronounced as Lady Calla and Lady Katherine Morrison.

The reception that follows this royal wedding is grander than anything anyone has ever seen besides the royal wedding of Queen Luana and Queen Consort Nona.

You may think this is the end, since they're all living happily ever after, and the bad guys have been caught, right?

No, this isn't the end.

This is only the beginning.

Later that night, while Katherine and Calla are asleep in their bed, a thought strikes Calla, and she bolts up in bed.

"Asmi escaped from prison."

"Calla? Baby, what is it? What's wrong?" Katherine asks groggily.

"Asmi escaped from prison. I must tell my stepfather at once. It's pretty early, so I'm sure he's in his office."

"Calla, are you insane? It's the middle of the night!"

"Honey, I'll be right back. Go back to sleep, unless you'd rather come with me."

"No, I think I'll stay warm and cozy under the covers."

Calla shakes her head at her new wife, and heads down the hall to her stepdad's office. She sees the light coming out from the bottom clearance, and she knocks on the door lightly.

"Who is it?"

"It's Calla, Dad."

"Come on in, Calla."

Calla enters her dad's office and sees him typing away.

"Working on something important, Dad?"

"Just something personal, my Lilly flower. Is everything alright?"

"Actually, no, Dad."

"What's the matter? Are you not feeling well?"

"I feel fine, Dad, it's just that Asmi was the one who kidnapped me. Somehow, and I don't know how, but they escaped from prison and kidnapped me, and they told me the end of the world will come sooner than we think."

"Slow down, Calla. Start again and say it slower."

Calla recounts slowly what she had previously said to her stepfather. Once she's finished, Kit pales a little.

"Dad, are *you* okay?"

"No, Calla. No, I'm not. We must send out word at once to Their Majesties."

"I wholeheartedly agree, Dad."

"Will you help me send out the message?"

"Of course, Dad."

The two send out the message through social media on a video post, saying that Asmi has escaped prison, is at large, and had kidnapped Calla. Once the message has been sent out to everyone, Kit's phone starts ringing off the hook.

"You go back to bed, kiddo. I'll take care of this."

"You sure?"

"Yes. There's nothing I can't handle, Calla. Go back to bed with your new wife."

"Okay. Thanks, Dad."

"You're welcome."

Calla heads back to bed, and Kit begins answering the many phone calls he has been receiving over the past few minutes.

The next morning, Kit knocks on his daughter and daughter-in-law's bedroom door, and Katherine sleepily opens it.

"Good morning, Kit. Oh, you look exhausted. Up late?"

"More like up *early,* Katie. I was busy answering phone calls till sunrise."

"All because Asmi kidnapped Calla?"

"It may not seem like that big of a deal to you, Katie, but –"

"Dad, don't say a word against my wife! Katherine knows this is a big deal, don't you, Katie?"

"I sure do, Calla."

"Forgive me for assuming anything, Katherine. I must be off to bed; I need to get at least a little bit of sleep before getting up for the day."

"We understand, Dad. Go get some sleep."

As soon as Kit is down the hall and in his room, Katie closes the door and she heads back to bed with her wife, their hands intertwined under the covers.

Soon, The Feast of the Goddess is upon them, and it's Katie and Calla's first holiday as a married couple.

But there's trouble amiss in the Hartreusian dungeon, as Kazamir is being interrogated by Luana's parents, Carter and Juniper, who have come out early from retirement in a cottage.

"Where is Asmi? Where are they, and why are you both so bent on kidnapping Calla?"

"It's simple. We want power."

"That's all?" Juniper nudges her husband.

"Well, you're not going to give it to me, are you?"

"No, we're not. Besides, we're no longer in power. Luana and Nona – oof!" Carter grunts after being elbowed in the ribs by Juniper.

"Interesting."

"We should have made sure *he* was the one being hanged, instead of that son of his."

"Temper, Carter, temper. You would do well to remember that *you* are no longer in power, but your daughter and daughter-in-law are. I guess I could stage a little accident for that daughter of yours, that way Nona would have no choice but to bow to me."

"And leave Emmalina alone, with no mothers to raise her?"

"So, she'll go back to the orphanage. So what? It's where she got her start, so why not make that her end as well?"

"Are you threatening our granddaughter?!" Carter asks.

"Certainly not, Carter. I wouldn't dream of it. But what I *am* doing is something very secret that no one, not even my child Asmi or boss Qhuvelia knows."

"And what is that, Kazamir?" Juniper asks.

"It's of no concern to you, Juniper. I'm done talking. I have no more to say to you."

"Very well. We'll come by if we have any more questions."

"I don't doubt you will."

With a sly smirk, Kazamir is escorted back to his prison cell, and Carter and Juniper head upstairs to talk to Luana and Nona.

"And you don't know where Asmi is? We never should have trusted them."

"It's not our fault, Lu. They seemed trusting at the time."

"While that may be true, the fact of the matter is that Asmi is still at large, and we have no idea where they could be, and we have no idea where to start."

"They could be at the ruins where Aunt Celeste and Uncle Kit got married? I mean, that's the first place *I* thought of." Emmalina says, stepping up to her two moms.

"That's not a bad idea, Emmalina." Carter says, ruffling his granddaughter's hair.

"Thank you, Granddad."

"You're welcome, kiddo. Luana, we should send some of the royal guard out to the ruins of the Indigonian manor."

"Wise decision, Dad. Richard?" Richard had been walking by the throne room when he heard Luana calling out to him.

"Yes, Your Majesty?"

"I need some of the royal guard to be sent out to the ruins of the Indigonian manor, and see if Asmi is there."

"Right away, Your Majesty."

"Thank you, Captain."

| 18 |

Kazamir Takes the Throne

The royal guard is sent out to try and find Asmi at the ruins of the Indigonian manor, but they are nowhere to be seen. So, the royal guard expands their search to the other parts of Gnypso, and they don't give up until the search seems hopeless and pointless. Defeated, the royal guard heads back to Hartreusia after giving Queen Luana and Queen Consort Nona a status update.

"Your Majesties, we couldn't locate Asmi, so there's no telling where they are."

"Very well. Return to Hartreusia at once, and make sure that you aren't – " The camera Luana is holding starts going staticky, and soon goes dark before coming back on, revealing Kazamir, and how he tied up the members of the Hartreusian royal family.

"Richard. Richard, Richard, Richard. How naïve of you to go off and find my child, when, really, they're gone. They've gone to a place that no one can find or reach, no matter what kind of powers they have. In the meantime, I've escaped from the Hartreusian dungeon and taken control of the throne. Come back home with your tails between your legs, boys. I do enjoy this."

The camera is abruptly shut off and the royal guard heads back to Hartreusia to save the Hartreusian royal family.

When they reach Hartreusia after a few days of riding, there's a riot outside the castle.

"People, please! Please part so we can get through and save the royal family."

"That's why we're here!"

"Please, let us do our jobs and protect the crown."

Kazamir suddenly comes out on the balcony at the front of the castle.

"Oh, it's too late for you to protect the crown. The royal family is locked up in the dungeon, and I've seized control of the throne."

"Not if we have any say in it." The townspeople say, grabbing their torches and pitchforks.

"Oh, dear. It seems that my child, Asmi, has returned from their long journey from...wherever it is that they went."

The rioters and the royal guard both turn to see Asmi holding a smoke bomb in one hand, and Emmalina by her hair in the other. The royal guard aims their bows and arrows at Asmi.

"Don't bother trying to defeat me. If you try to shoot me, Emmalina will be used as a human shield."

"Stand down, men. We can't risk hitting the crown princess."

"Very good, Richard. We wouldn't want the sole inheritor to be left to die, now, would we?"

The royal guard puts down their bows and arrows, and Emmalina squirms from her place in Asmi's grasp.

"Don't squirm, little one. Right now, my dear father is holding your parents and grandparents hostage, and there's no one that can stop him, not even the royal guard."

Richard looks back at the rioters and nods, knowing that the townspeople are the only ones who can save the Atteberrys.

"Oh, I must be off. I have a bargain to settle with Aileen."

"T-the goddess of all beings, living and dead?"

"Yes."

"HEY! Unhand my cousin right now!" Asmi turns and sees Calla approaching with her own royal guard.

"Let her go. Now. Asmi, you're better than this. You don't have to serve Qhuvelia anymore."

"Why should I listen to you, Calla? You'll only turn me in to the royal guard."

"And why would that be a bad thing? You've been sentenced to life in prison because of you killing Hazel."

"Oh, details, details. Everyone knows that Hazel doesn't truly exist, but that Aileen took the form of her so you would know that you are the chosen one to save us all from the end of the world. She died before she could tell you."

"W-what are you talking about, Asmi?"

"Don't pretend you don't know about Aileen being disguised as Hazel, who never truly existed."

"I wasn't talking about that. I was talking about me being the chosen one. Does everyone – does everyone know I'm meant to be the chosen one?"

"It's no secret, Calla. You were foretold by Aileen herself, that you would save us from ourselves. You're a legend, and a myth, all rolled into one small girl."

"Why should I believe you?"

"Because they're telling the truth, little Calla." Calla turns and sees Aileen walking towards the people of Hartreusia.

"Aileen?"

"It is me, child. I believe that you kept your end of the bargain."

"Bargain? What bargain?"

"The bargain that will give you the choice of a lifetime."

"What choice?"

"Either you come with me and live in paradise in the Broken Realm, or I step down as the allmother and become Hazel once again."

"And leave my family behind?"

"I thought you'd say that. Very well. I will step down, put one of my children in charge of the Broken Realm, so I, as Hazel, can help you train for the end of the world. It's busy up there in the Broken Realm, bringing about the end of worlds in different galaxies, *and* watching over the people of Gnypso."

"Wait. You'd really step down from your position as the allmother? For *me?*"

"Yes, Calla. I created you in my image, because when your father impregnated your mother, I saw something special in you from the moment you were conceived."

"And you really believe that I'm someone special, Aileen?"

"I don't just believe it, little one. I *know.*"

"I think I understand now."

"Good. I will put Era in charge of the Broken Realm. Give me a moment."

In a flash of blinding light, Aileen disappears and is gone. A moment later, and not a moment sooner, Aileen returns and transforms from the all-powerful allmother into the not-as-powerful human Hazel.

"I'm back, baby! No one can replace your Grandma Hazel, now can they?"

Calla runs forward and hugs her Grandma Hazel.

"I'm here, child. Don't worry. I'm not going anywhere ever again, I can guarantee that. You can't get rid of me that easily."

"I wouldn't *want* to get rid of you, Grandma Hazel."

"I am so glad to hear that, Calla. Now, Asmi, let go of Emmalina. Or would you rather I smite you where you stand?"

"No, no, Hazel. That won't be necessary. I'll – I'll let her go." Asmi lets Emmalina go and she runs to Hazel.

"Don't you worry, Princess. We'll make sure your parents and grandparents are going to be safe and sound and not held captive by Kazamir."

"Grandma Hazel?" Calla asks.

"What is it, child?"

"Can I ask you something?"

"Of course!"

"Is Kazamir your son, or was that just a ploy?"

"Kazamir really is my son. I cast him out of the Broken Realm for threatening to join my sister Qhuvelia."

"But he actually joined her."

"Yes, I'm quite aware of that, Calla. Better to be safe, than sorry, am I right?"

"Of course, Hazel."

"Kazzy! You let the royal peoples go at once, or will I have to come up there and smite you?"

"You don't scare me, you old crone."

Hazel goes up to Kazamir and transforms into the allmother Aileen, and she slaps Kazamir across his face before turning back into Hazel.

"Don't make me smite you, Kevin. A slap across a face will be the least of your worries once I get through with you."

"I-I'm sorry, Mother. I was just jealous of the power that everyone I know has. You know, the powers you and Asmi have...those skipped my generation."

"Yes, but every child you've ever had has powers, regardless of who their mother is."

"I understand, Mother."

"Good. Now let the Atteberrys go. Please, Kazamir. I wouldn't want you to be hurt. You may be a criminal, but you're still my baby boy."

"Yes, Mother."

Kazamir, with Hazel's supervision, unties the royal family and turns them loose.

Emmalina runs through the crowd and embraces her parents and grandparents.

All is well.

| 19 |

Hazel's Secret

The charges against Asmi for the first-degree murder of Hazel have been dropped, since Hazel was Aileen all along, and, thus, cannot be killed because of her status as a goddess.

Life seems to go back to normal...well, as normal as it can for the Gnypsonians.

A year later, Calla, her wife Katherine, and Calla's two sisters, Victoria and Celeste, and Hazel, are at the latter's hut looking through old photo albums of Hazel's.

"I can't believe you used to be a royal, Hazel." Calla says as she sees pictures of Hazel from centuries ago.

"It's true. I had a double-job: I was both a deity and a lady of Lavenderia."

"That sounds like a lot of work, Grandma Hazel." Not-So-Little Celeste says.

"It was more work than you'd think, kiddo. But no one outside of our little group can know that I was once a royal. I wouldn't want anyone to treat me any differently than they already do, considering the fact that they know my true identity."

Once the girls are all finished looking through the photo albums, Hazel and the girls fix her famous summer stew.

"No one makes it like you, Hazel. Believe me, I've tried. Katie, remember when we tried to make it for the beginning-of-the-school-year feast?"

"I do." Katie tells her wife.

"It was alright, but it was missing Hazel's magic touch."

"Welp, it's getting late, kids. I'd best send you all home with some of my summer stew."

"Awwwww."

"Don't 'awwwww' me, girls. It's about time you headed home for the night. I'll come by tomorrow so we can spend some time together."

"Thank you, Grandma Hazel."

"And don't tell anyone that I was a royal. Like I said, no one needs to treat me any differently than they already do."

"We understand, Grandma Hazel. But why did you give up your title?"

"That's a story I'm afraid I can't tell you. Now skedaddle! It's getting late, and I don't want you gals out after sundown if you can help it."

"Yes, Grandma Hazel."

The girls head out to their horses with some of Hazel's summer stew and head home after waving to Hazel.

Content, Hazel heads back inside her hut.

"Asmi, you can come out now."

"Forgive me, Hazel. I just don't think those girls trust me again yet."

"Well, can you really blame them, Asmi? You were thought to have murdered me."

"So, you faked your death, making poor Calla develop PTSD and need a service dog."

"Yes, I did. I didn't expect Calla to be so traumatized."

"But you're all-knowing."

"As Aileen, I'm all-knowing. As Hazel, I'm limited with what I know. The line between my two identities is blurry, and there are advantages and disadvantages to having two identities, one of them immortal and the other, well, not *as* immortal."

"I see."

"I can't be killed, Asmi, even though many people have tried."

"I don't understand, Hazel. Why fake your own death?"

"To tell you the truth, Asmi, I was getting tired of being a human. After some time, you become weak as a human, and, even though I'm an all-powerful goddess, my powers were diminishing. So, to fool everyone, I faked my death, sacrificing myself for Celeste. When in reality, I just transferred some of my power to Celeste so she wouldn't be in any more pain in the Broken Realm. Part of me wishes I had just told Calla and Katie the truth about what I did, instead of faking my death. The poor girls will probably be traumatized for life, and I have only myself to blame. And I'm sorry, Asmi, you had to spend so much time behind bars."

"I don't blame you, Hazel. You fooled even me, and I'm a good trickster."

"You get that from me, Asmi. Now, let me fix up some of my stew for you so you can be on your way back to Hartreusia."

"I still can't believe I get to be the royal advisor once again."

"Hey, once the charges were dropped, you could have had your pick of any job in the entire world. So, why become the royal advisor again?"

"Because it's good money...but, in all seriousness, working for Their Majesties is the best job an ex-convict like me could ever have."

"And why is that?"

"Because I've always loved the royal family. Ever since I was in the orphanage, I've always thought I would be adopted by the Atteberrys, but when Queen Luana and Queen Consort Nona adopted Emmalina, I became a little jealous they had picked her to adopt instead of me. But, eventually, I got over it. Emmalina's a good girl, and she deserves a good family."

"So do you, Asmi."

"Well, I've got the girls to help look after, and I've got you, and the royals. I couldn't ask for a better chosen family."

"I'm sure you couldn't. Now, off to Hartreusia you go. If you need me, give me a call."

"I will, Hazel, and thank you for being so hospitable."

"You're quite welcome, Asmi."

Asmi smiles and nods at Hazel, and then they head out with a satchel full of bread and Hazel's summer stew.

Once Asmi reaches Hartreusia from Lavenderia a few days later, most everyone is greeting them with smiles and good words. But some, still bitter about Hazel's supposed death, give them glares and harsh words. Asmi ignores the latter and continues on their way to the Hartreusian palace.

They reach the palace and head to the back stables to dismount and give their horse to be tacked up. Once that's done, Asmi heads into the palace to the library, where Their Majesties are just reading and having quiet moments by themselves for a while.

"Queen Luana? Queen Consort Nona?"

"Asmi! What brings you here? Ah, don't tell us. You're here because you want that job of royal advisor again, don't you?" Nona asks.

"How did you know?"

"Wild guess. And Hazel texted me, telling me that you wanted the job again. As a matter of fact, Luana just told me she gave you back your old advisor job."

"She did?"

"She did."

"A thousand thank you's, Queen Luana. I won't let you down."

"We'll hold you to it, Asmi. Now, off with you. My wife and I have some reading to do, unless you'd like to join us."

"My apologies, Your Majesty, but I'd rather get some sleep. It was a long journey from Lavenderia back home to Hartreusia."

"Not a problem, Asmi. We wish you have pleasant dreams, and we bid you good night."

"Thank you kindly, Queen Consort Nona. It means the world to me."

Asmi leaves the library and, although they had told the queens they were heading to bed, they really head to the dungeons to see Kazamir.

"Richard, I'm here to speak with my father."

"Of course, Asmi. But I'm afraid Kazamir is not accepting visitors at the moment."

"And why not?"

"Because he simply does not want visitors. He's in a bit of a foul mood."

"Any particular reason?"

"Not that I'm aware of, Asmi. It must be the weather or something in the air."

"Alright. Will you inform me as soon as – "

There's suddenly a clatter and a clang heard from Kazamir's cell.

"What was that?"

"I don't know, but I've got a bad feeling, Richard."

"Me, too. Let's go."

Asmi and Richard cautiously and carefully head towards Kazamir's cell, and, as soon as they peer around the corner, Richard immediately goes to open the cell door.

"Asmi, run as fast as you can and get the healer. Kazamir has collapsed."

Asmi nods and runs as fast as they can to get the royal healer.

When Asmi comes back with the healer, Richard is the one unconscious with the cell door wide open.

"Kazamir's escaped. Inform the royal family and the royal guard at once!" Asmi exclaims to Ciara, who had appeared near Asmi after hearing the commotion of Kazamir's escape.

"Right away, Asmi."

The queens head down to the dungeons to see Asmi pacing, wondering where their father could have gone.

"Your Majesties, I had a bad feeling, but I didn't know it was that he had escaped. I knew something was wrong, I just didn't know what that was."

"Don't blame yourself, Asmi. This is not your doing, only Kazamir's to blame here."

"I understand, Queen Consort Nona. But that, unfortunately, doesn't really make me feel any better."

"That's understandable. You used to work for Kazamir, did you not?"

"In a way, Queen Luana, yes, I did."

"We must send out an announcement saying that Kazamir has escaped once again. Ciara?"

"Right away, Your Majesty. I'll make the announcement myself. Care to join me in making the announcement, Asmi?"

"Of course, Ciara."

Ciara and Asmi head to the royal study, where they set up a camera and make the announcement.

"Attention, all Gnypsonians: Asmi and I are afraid we have distressing news. Kazamir has escaped from the royal dungeons of Hartreusia. Please be on your guard, and anyone found helping him, will be charged with holding a convict within their residence or place of business. Thank you, and have a good evening."

Meanwhile, Kazamir is running through the woods of Lavenderia, hoping to reach one place, and one place alone: his mother's hut.

"Mother...Hazel...I must speak with you at once."

"What business do you have to darken my doorway, Kazamir Riker?"

"My only business I have here is to ask for forgiveness from the allmother, and my own mother."

"We are one and the same, Kazamir. But, as you wish, I will transform into my true self."

In a flash of golden light, Hazel transforms into her human self into her goddess persona.

"Why should I even *think* about forgiving you, my son? I am not that a benevolent goddess. I am all-powerful, and all-knowing, yes, but I am not all-forgiving."

"I ask not for forgiveness just from you, Aileen, but from my mother Hazel, as well. I have done you both wrong, and I wish to repent for my mistakes."

"Give me a few days to think about it." Suddenly, Aileen sputters.

"Why should I even be harboring you, my son? You are a wanted criminal."

"While that may be true, Aileen, you are not going to be punished for harboring me. You are a goddess, and the allmother at that. No one can touch you."

"While it is correct and true that I am the allmother, I *can*, in fact, be touched by the law, and those that write the laws."

"So, *law*makers?"

"Don't get snide with me, Kazamir. I may be the mother of all, but, first and foremost, and I mean this in the very best way possible, I am *your* mother."

"Oh, what should I do?"

"Turn yourself in."

"Mother, I'm serious."

"As am I, son."

"But to go back to the Hartreusian dungeon for the umpteenth time...who knows what they'll do to me?"

"I do, Kazamir. If you turn yourself in, I'm sure Queen Luana and Queen Consort Nona will make sure your punishment is less than severe."

"Please, Mother. Don't turn me in."

"It's not up to me."

"But you are the *allmother*."

"While I am the allmother, I am first and foremost *your* mother, and I will not tolerate you running from the law. So, either turn yourself in, or I will do it for you."

"Mother, you can't do this!"

"I can, and I will, but only if you give me no choice here, Kazamir. Please. Don't make this harder than it has to be."

Kazamir closes his eyes and thinks back to all the memories he's had with his mother over the years. When he opens them, they're full of tears.

"I will turn myself in, but only for you, Mother. I will make sure I serve my full sentence and come to take care of you. I promise."

"We'll see what comes next for you, Kazamir."

There's suddenly a knock on the door and Aileen goes to open it. The guards tremble in awe before the allmother, kissing the ground where she walks.

"You've come to retrieve my son, have you not?"

"Yes, Your Holiness."

"Very well. Kazamir, please step forward."

Once Kazamir steps forward, he's immediately tackled by the royal guard, shackled and put in the prison carriage, off to Hartreusia. Kazamir looks back at his mother, and she looks back at him wistfully. She closes the door behind her and goes to prepare her next meal for the day. Alone.

Meanwhile, the ladies of Rosiary are with their families in the Morrison estate, just enjoying one another's company, despite the threat of Kazamir having escaped looming over their heads.

"Oh, I do hope Kazamir is caught soon, and that Hazel isn't harmed too much by him, if he were to go to her."

"Hazel can handle herself. She's the allmother for...well, for her sake!"

"I do know that when she relinquished some of her power to save my mum, she made it look like she sacrificed herself, when, really, she was as fit as a fiddle then as she is now."

"Yes, it is quite spectacular that she only gave up some of her power to save your mum, and didn't end up sacrificing her whole self for her. Or for you." Victoria says.

"Girls?" Kit asks, knocking on the door of Calla and Katie's room.

"Yes, Dad?"

"Kazamir has been caught and is being escorted by prison carriage back to the Hartreusian dungeon as we speak."

"Oh, thank the Broken Realm! I'm so glad to hear that!"

"I am, too, Calla. We're all having a celebratory dinner tonight in honor of Kazamir's capture."

The girls head downstairs with Kit and head to dinner. Once everyone – Inge, Kit, Emmitt, Isabella, Calla, Victoria, Celeste, and Katie – is seated in their own chairs, dinner is served and the chatter begins.

"I can't believe that Kazamir escaped and was captured so quickly. To think he started out as a lowly player, and now look where that's gotten him." Emmitt says.

"And being a player is something you should never aspire to be. Right, Dad?"

"That's right, Victoria."

"I still can't believe that Calla has been kidnapped multiple times throughout her life."

"*I* can't believe you're bringing that up, Celeste. And about your own sister?"

"Very well, Mum. I won't say any more about Calla being kidnapped."

"That's our good girl. Now, eat your vegetables, girls, so you can grow big and strong."

"Like we aren't already big." Victoria mutters. The young girls laugh at this before Isabella shoots them all a scolding look.

The chatter continues, and, on another part of Gnypso, Asmi is heading down to speak with his father.

"I wish to speak with Kazamir."

"He was just brought back in, Asmi. One moment, please." "Take all the time you need, Captain."

Asmi soon sits in a chair across from his father.

"Kazamir, you must be wondering why I'm here."

"I am."

"Well, the truth of the matter is that I want to make you a deal."

"What kind of a deal?"

"The kind that will benefit the both of us."

"I'm listening."

"I think that everyone would benefit from one thing: bringing down the monarchy."

"Oh? And why would you want to help me do that? You just got back into the position as the Atteberry family's royal advisor."

"It was all a trick to get them to trust me again. With the charges dropped and Hazel still alive and well, I had no choice but to start plotting my revenge on the very family that is holding my father hostage."

"And why should I let you help me? I'm going to be stuck in the dungeon for the rest of my life."

"While that's true, I have a plan involving Qhuvelia herself."

"And what plan might that be?"

"The plan to end the world as we know it, and destroy the monarchy."

"I like the way you think, Asmi."

"I thought you might. Now, you do exactly as I tell you to do, and you'll have your day in court and be sentenced to community service or something. Something less severe than life in prison."

| 20 |

Asmi's Plan

Once upon a time, in a land far, far away, there lived an orphan called Asmi. Asmi was a brilliantly smart child, but that led to them not having many friends in the orphanage, except for one: a little girl called Emmalina.

The two became inseparable, but, one day, long after Asmi had moved out of the orphanage to find their place in the world, Luana and Nona came to the orphanage to adopt someone, and they ended up choosing Emmalina. Asmi heard of this news, considering that Emmalina was soon to become the crown princess of Hartreusia, and of Gnypso, and they became bitter, because they didn't become the child of the monarch.

During that years-long wait, Asmi had started working for Qhuvelia, and soon moved up in rank, becoming her second-in-command, making them Kazamir's boss, alongside Qhuvelia.

After some time in the Hartreusian dungeon, Asmi defected back to the good side after learning of Hazel's true identity, but then defected back to the bad side because they, too, wanted power, and still do.

And so, Asmi came up with a plan to take down the monarchy, working undercover as the royal advisor. They knew that both Luana and Nona have one weakness – their daughter, Emmalina. Doing something nonlethal to Emmalina would make them bow down to both Asmi *and* Kazamir.

Therefore, Asmi's plan is about to take place.

It's the middle of the night in the Hartreusian castle, and, although Asmi had kidnapped Calla, they were let off on the kidnapping charge because Calla didn't press charges, since she was found safe and sound by Aileen. Asmi is roaming the castle at around 1AM when they see Emmalina creeping down the stairs to go to the kitchen for a late-night snack.

Emmalina grabs an apple with caramel from the refrigerator, and she moves to head back to her room, but Asmi is quick and stops her.

"It's a bit late for a snack, don't you think, Princess?"

"I know it's late, Auncle Asmi, but I woke up hungry, so I decided to get a snack."

"I noticed you didn't eat much at dinner."

"My stomach was kind of hurting, which was weird...but I went to the bathroom, and I found blood in my underwear."

"Ah. You must have gotten your first period."

"Oh, yes. Calla told me about her first period. I guess it was time for me to get mine."

"Let me escort you back to your room, Your Highness. I was getting up for my daily jog anyway."

"At 1 in the morning? Odd."

"I like to stretch and do yoga. I go to bed early, so I can get up early."

Emmalina looks a bit puzzled at her auncle, but she follows them, but they pass right by the staircase.

"Why aren't we going up to my room?"

"Well, I just thought we'd take a little stroll out to the stables, see how the new foal is doing."

"There's a new foal?"

"Yes, there is. And she's quite the spunky little filly, a lot like you, Princess." Asmi says, tapping Emmalina's nose lightly.

Inside, Asmi is feeling more and more guilty about their plan to kidnap the crown princess. But they feel it must be done for the sake of Qhuvelia. And so, after Asmi lures Emmalina out to the stables to see the new filly, they knock her unconscious with a bale of hay.

When Emmalina wakes up, she's in a place that is familiar to her.

"Mmmm?"

"Oh, you're awake, Princess. We were afraid you didn't make it."

"G-Grandma Hazel?"

"I'm here, child. And your Auncle Asmi is here, too."

"They are?"

"Yes. I'm here, Emmalina."

"What happened?"

"I – I lured you out to the stable, and, while you were fawning over the filly, I knocked you unconscious with a bale of hay. I'm afraid that I did this for Qhuvelia."

"So, you did it all for the goddess of the underworld?"

"I'm afraid so, little Emmalina."

"Why?"

"Because I wanted what you have."

"Love?"

"No. Power. Because I want to rule as sovereign. But I'm afraid I'll never get there because I kidnapped the crown princess of Hartreusia."

"You could always say that I willingly went with you."

"Yes, but that wouldn't be the truth, Emmalina. I wouldn't want to perjure myself in front of the entire world."

"So...there's nothing I can do to stop you from getting arrested and sent back to prison?"

"Well, unless you drop the charges, there's nothing really that you can do. But I'm afraid you can't drop the charges."

"And why not?"

"Because you're not even 13 yet, plus you are still a minor. The only person or people that can drop the charges against me would be either one or both of your mums."

"I understand, Auncle Asmi."

"I'm glad you do."

"Shall we go back to Hartreusia and see if my mums will drop the charges?"

"We'll have to see whether or not they'll do just that. Come. Let's go home."

"Okay."

With Hazel's summer stew packed up for the journey home, Asmi and Emmalina mount a horse and ride home. It takes them a few days to get from Lavenderia to Hartreusia, but, once they get there, the royal guard immediately takes Asmi into custody.

"Emmalina! We're so glad you're alright! Are you hurt?" Nona asks her daughter.

"No, Mum. I'm fine. In fact, I – I don't want to press charges against Auncle Asmi."

"Well, I'm afraid that's not your decision, Emmalina. You're still a minor, and you can't make important decisions like that."

"Can't you make it for me, Mama?"

"Even though I'm queen, it would not be wise to drop charges against the criminal who kidnapped the crown princess of Hartreusia." Luana replies.

"But what if I don't *want* charges pressed against them?"

"Like I said, Emmalina, that's not your decision to make. I'm sorry. Mum's and my hands are tied."

"It's not fair. Auncle Asmi only did it to please Qhuvelia."

"I'm afraid life isn't fair, sweetheart. And even though they did it to please Qhuvelia, they still did it regardless, and, thus, charges cannot be dropped."

"Once I'm queen, I'll drop the charges against Asmi."

"Once you're queen, they may be out of prison by then, or you'll have grown up and realized that what we did arresting them was the right thing to do."

"What if once I'm queen, and they're not out of prison, I still want to drop the charges?"

"Well, then, that will be the decision that *you,* and you alone, have to make for yourself and for your Auncle Asmi."

"I understand. I'm tired, can I go to bed now?"

"Since you were hit on the head, we want the royal healer to examine you. And, if all is well, then you can go to bed."

"Alright. Oh, and by the way, I got my first period."

"You did?"

"I did."

"Congratulations, sweetheart."

"Thank you."

"You're welcome. Come on. Let's go get you examined by the royal healer."

The royal healer soon examines Emmalina, and gives her a clean bill of health, except for a slight concussion.

"I suggest rest and no hard work for the next few weeks."

"Thank you."

"You're welcome, Your Majesty."

Emmalina and her two moms leave the healer's office and Emmalina is sent up to bed, being carefully watched by Nona.

A few weeks pass, and Emmalina is cleared by the royal healer, and she is set to testify against Asmi in the royal court.

"Princess Emmalina, is it true that you were lured out to the stables to see the newborn filly?"

"Yes."

"And is it true you were wandering the castle of your own volition at 1 o'clock in the morning?"

"Yes. I was hungry, so I went down to grab a snack – some apple slices with caramel."

"And did Asmi trick you into believing that you were just going out to see the new filly?"

"Yes, that is accurate."

"And did Asmi, while you were looking at the filly, then knock you unconscious with this bale of hay?" The attorney shows the picture of the bale of hay that was used to knock the princess unconscious.

"Yes."

"No further questions, Your Highness."

"The plaintiff may step down. Counselor, call your next person to the stand."

"I call Asmi to the stand."

Asmi steps up, takes the oath, and sits down.

"Asmi, why were you up at 1 o'clock in the morning?"

"I was trying to think of how to lure the princess out so I could knock her unconscious."

"And what was the excuse that you came up with to lure the princess?"

"That I was getting ready for my morning jog by stretching and doing yoga. I told the princess that I go to bed early so I can wake up early."

"Yes, but at 1 in the morning?"

"I see your point, counselor."

"Asmi, is it true that you work for the goddess of the under-world?"

"Yes. I'm actually Qhuvelia's second-in-command, even above my father, Kazamir. He also works for her."

"No further questions."

"Asmi, you may step down from the stand. Counselor, any more people to ask questions?"

"No, Your Honor."

"Then court is dismissed until the jury has reached a verdict."

A few weeks later, the jury has reached a verdict on whether Asmi will be, once again, sentenced to life in prison, with no bail or probation.

"Has the jury reached a verdict?"

"We have, Your Honor."

"On the count of child endangerment, how do you find?"

"We find Asmi guilty of child endangerment."

"On the count of kidnapping, how do you find?

"We find Asmi guilty of kidnapping."

"Very well. Asmi, you are sentenced to life in prison, with no chances of bail or probation."

"I understand, Your Honor."

"Guards, please escort Asmi into the dungeon."

The guards do just that, and Asmi is taken into custody.

| 21 |

Six Years Later

Six years have passed since Asmi's sentencing, and it's nearly coronation day for Emmalina to become queen.

There's a hustle and bustle around the Atteberry castle, and Emmalina is with her cousins, Victoria, Celeste, Calla and Katherine, getting her final dress fitting done before the coronation.

"You look absolutely beautiful, Emmalina." Calla tells her cousin.

"Thank you, Lady Calla. It means so much to me that you all are here to celebrate little old me."

"We wouldn't want to be anywhere else. Have you made the decision on whether to drop the charges against Asmi as your first thing to do as queen of Hartreusia?"

"I have, and I've decided to drop the charges. They don't deserve to have life in prison when I was so easily lured in my youth."

There's suddenly a commotion outside the door of the seamstress' quarters.

"Emmalina, stay here. We'll check it out. Katie, you stay here as well. With your condition, you shouldn't be under too much stress."

"I'll watch Emmalina like a hawk, Calla." Katherine says, caressing her baby bump.

"Good. We'll be back soon, my love."

As soon as Calla, Victoria and Celeste are outside the seamstress' quarters, Katie sits down in a chair, utterly exhausted from carrying a baby for the past seven months, Emmalina joins her, equally as exhausted from planning her coronation.

Soon, Calla peeks her head back into the room, smiling at the seamstress, Katie and Emmalina.

"It's alright, you three. The coast is clear."

"What happened?"

"It seems that Kazamir and Asmi have both tried to escape from the royal dungeons...again."

"We really need to up the security in the dungeon."

"Well, with Asmi's powers, getting outside the castle grounds would have been easy for them both."

"It shouldn't be that way, but it is." Victoria says as she and her two sisters come back into the room.

"I believe the thing I do after I become queen, after pardoning Asmi, is tightening down on the royal guard. It shouldn't be this easy for Kazamir and Asmi to escape. Calla, write this down." Calla grabs a piece of parchment paper and a quill with ink.

"We need to come up with a device to make sure that Asmi's powers can't be used to aid their and Kazamir's escape."

"Agreed, Emmalina."

"Girls? Are you alright?"

"We're fine, Mum!" Emmalina calls back to Nona.

"That's good to hear! It's almost time for your coronation, so your cousins will need to leave to go get ready."

"Yes, Mum!" As soon as Nona's footsteps fade away, Emmalina turns to the girls.

"Not a word of my pardoning Asmi to anyone, girls. Is that understood?"

"Of course, Emmalina."

"Good. Now, shoo. I must finish getting ready for my coronation, and I suggest you all do the same."

Katie, Calla, Victoria and Celeste all curtsy to their soon-to-be-queen, then leave to get ready for the event.

As soon as the girls have left Emmalina and the seamstress alone, the two get to talking.

"Laurel, do you really think I'm fit to be queen?"

"Oh, of course, Your Highness. No one is more prepared for the job than you are."

"I know I'm *physically* prepared, but what if I'm not *emotionally* prepared?"

"You just take your being queen one day at a time, Your Highness.."

"Thank you for the advice, Laurel."

"You're welcome. Now, let me look at you in your finest gown. It's quite the replica of the one you wore when you became princess. Are you ready to become queen of Hartreusia, and of Gnypso?"

"I am."

Soon, Emmalina walks down the aisle to the front of the throne room, where her parents and grandparents are waiting for her to step up and take her place as the next queen of Hartreusia.

Emmalina, in all her years here in the Atteberry castle, has not found her true love, but she hopes that some suitors will come her way whenever she feels ready to begin courting her future spouse.

Emmalina is coronated as queen as the chorus sings a song about the queens from the past. After she is coronated, the ball is as grand as can be.

There's dancing, a great feast and songs that are sung celebrating the new queen.

After the ball ends around midnight, Emmalina heads to bed, full of good food and good memories made with friends and family.

The next morning, Emmalina goes down to the dungeon to see Asmi.

"Richard? I'd like to speak with Asmi, please."

"Right away, Queen Emmalina. I must say, Your Majesty, your new title really rolls off the tongue."

"Thank you for saying so, Richard."

"You're welcome, Your Highness. If you'll follow me, please."

Emmalina nods and she follows the captain of the royal guard to Asmi's cell. They're currently asleep.

"On your feet, Asmi. Her Majesty would like a word with you."

"If I must, Richard."

"Yes, you must."

"And why has the brand-new queen of Hartreusia come to see me?"

"I'd like to actually speak with you in private, Asmi. Richard?"

"I'll be nearby, Your Majesty."

"I don't doubt it, Captain."

As soon as Richard is out of earshot, Emmalina lowers her voice so she and Asmi will not be overheard.

"I'd like my first duty as queen to be pardoning you."

"And why would you want to do a silly thing like that? I kidnapped you. I deserve to rot in here."

"You didn't truly mean me any harm, Asmi, and I believe that you deserve to be set free."

"You truly believe that, Your Majesty?"

"I do. But on one condition."

"And what is that?"

"You don't kidnap anyone for as long as you live, and don't cause anymore trouble."

Asmi sighs before speaking.

"I accept and agree to your terms."

"Good. Richard?"

"Yes, Queen Emmalina?"

"Set Asmi free."

"Y-Your Majesty, are you certain that's what you want to do?"

"I'm the queen, aren't I? I have that power, don't I?"

"Well, yes, you do, Queen Emmalina, but Asmi – they're a dangerous person."

"They've agreed to my terms of not kidnapping anyone for as long as they live, and not causing any more trouble."

"And you're really going to hold them to that?"

"Yes. I believe there's still good in my Auncle Asmi."

"Very well, Your Majesty." Richard unlocks the cell door and lets Asmi walk out before they leave the castle, seemingly for good.

"A thousand thank you's, Queen Emmalina. If there's anything else I can do to make it up to you, please don't hesitate to ask me."

"Just go, Asmi. You've irritated the Atteberry royal family enough."

"Yes, Your Highness." Asmi says, slightly hurt at the new queen's words towards them. They do their bow-curtsy combination before leaving the castle grounds.

When Asmi leaves, and the royal guard watches them leave, they look back at the castle one final time.

| 22 |

The New Generation

Two months after Emmalina's coronation, Calla and Katie welcome a new baby into the world – a son they named Jehan Tobias.

Jehan grows up in a home filled with love. Faith, now retired as a service dog and is now a family dog, loves Jehan, and lets him grab her ears and tail, but nips him gently if he pulls too hard in his babyhood. Calla is no longer in need of a service dog, as her PTSD is now much more manageable.

Once Jehan becomes a toddler, he talks a lot with his nanny Alison, along with his two mothers, his three sets of grandparents, and two aunts.

Everyone is careful not to let Jehan get into too much trouble, and Asmi, now reformed, comes to visit as often as they can, wanting to make amends with everyone for the kidnappings. It's been two months since Asmi was set free, and they haven't kidnapped anyone since their release from prison. However, Kazamir is still in prison, and will remain there for the rest of his days. Queen Emmalina did not take kindly to him being so mean over the years.

Hazel comes to visit her great-great-grandson as much as she can, and spoils him rotten with good food, good toys and good books. Jehan is practically raised on Hazel's summer stew.

All seems to be well, until Kazamir, once again, escapes from the Hartreusian royal dungeon with the help of Qhuvelia herself.

Hazel prepares herself to battle both her sister and her son, but Calla, Katherine and Kit all stop her before she takes on more than she can handle, even as the all-powerful allmother.

Once Kazamir seems to be in Rosiary, the whole country goes on lockdown, closing businesses and schoolhouses, to keep everyone safe and sound.

The Morrisons and Villareals start to all go stir-crazy, being cooped up inside for a few weeks.

They video chat with their relatives and friends in the other countries of Gnypso: the Atteberrys in Hartreusia, the other Morrisons in Eburnean, Holly and Julia in Lavenderia, and Kessia and her wife Lucy in Indigonia.

Fruitless searches for Kazamir pass by the Gnypsonians, and years pass by as well.

Jehan is a young adult now, and has enlisted in the Hartreusian royal guard.

Once he enlists, Jehan begins packing up his things with his mothers' help.

The packing takes at least a day and a half, and, when packing has completed, Calla and Katherine see their son off to Hartreusia to begin basic training.

There are tears for everyone, including Asmi, when Jehan leaves, and there are hugs to and from Jehan and everyone.

Jehan leaves, and soon, he reaches the Hartreusian castle.

Back in Rosiary, Calla and her two sisters, Victoria and Celeste, all of them all grown up now, take a trip to A Likely Story, just like old times.

They reach the bookshop, and head inside to browse for some new reading material. They plan on hitting the ice cream shop, Big Scoops, after their book-shopping trip.

Emmalina sits on her throne in the Hartreusian castle, trying her best to stay awake as she listens to the townspeople's complaints, concerns, and suggestions.

Soon, the townspeople leave their queen to be by herself. Courting will soon begin for the queen, as she hasn't really dated anyone in the past eighteen years. With the recent death of her grandfather, Carter, she believes that life is too short to spend it alone.

So, she enlists the help of her surviving grandmother Juniper, and her mothers, Luana and Nona, to help her choose a suitor worthy enough to rule by her side as king, queen or sovereign.

Suitors from all different walks of life and from all over Gnypso come to try and court their queen, to make her their own personal queen.

But, in the end, only one of the suitors strikes Emmalina's fancy: a young woman by the name of Adelaide. Born as a commoner and spell caster, Adelaide doesn't know much about royalty except what she's heard of in old stories and read of in books.

Adelaide and Emmalina, from the moment they first saw each other in person, are inseparable, and they don't want to spend another moment without one another. Months pass from the beginning of courting, and Adelaide and Emmalina both plan on proposing to each other after knowing each other for almost a year.

One evening, while Emmalina and Adelaide are out for a stroll in the garden, they both realize that they're being watched from inside the castle.

Emmalina and Adelaide sit down on one of the benches in one of the gazebos.

"Adelaide, my dearest, dearest Adelaide. I've been thinking about us, and I wanted to ask you: how would you like to be not only the queen consort of Hartreusia and Gnypso, but also the queen of my heart?"

"You truly mean that, Emmalina?"

"I do."

"Well, then, Emmalina. Yes, I would love to be the queen of your heart. I guess that is you asking me to marry you?"

"Yes. And I-I picked out a ring and bought it with my own money, not with money from the vault."

"May I see it?"

"Oh, yes. Yes, of course." Emmalina takes out the ring and presents it to Adelaide. It's a gold halo ring with a circle-shaped diamond and little diamonds around the big one.

"Oh, Emmalina. It's beautiful."

"So, is that a yes?"

"That's a *heck yes!*"

"I am very pleased to hear that."

Emmalina and Adelaide kiss, and wedding planning soon comes and goes. The wedding ceremony and reception are the grandest party in the history of the planet Gnypso: everyone from all walks of life, all places on Gnypso, attend the most royal of royal weddings.

Jehan is moving up in rank as a royal guard of Hartreusia.

Calla and Katherine are expecting a little girl, that they are going to name Astrid June.

She arrives, screaming her little lungs out, pink and as healthy as can be.

The newest member of the Morrison family is fawned over and cooed over by all who encounter her.

She's a girl worth waiting for, and no one can ever say "no" to her.

Even more years pass, and Astrid is the spitting image of both of her mothers, since she was conceived by splicing an egg of Calla's and an egg of Katherine's and was fertilized by an anonymous donor.

Astrid's fifth birthday soon rolls around, and she is, once again, fawned over and cooed over by all of her birthday ball guests.

During the party, Calla, Katherine, Victoria and Celeste all sneak away to look again at Hazel's photo albums, to try and find out why Hazel gave up her title, since they remembered that she had told them not to tell anyone that Hazel was once a royal.

While they're looking in the albums, Jehan knocks on the door to find his mothers and aunts looking at the old album.

"Mama? Mum? It's time for Astrid to open her presents."

"We'll be right down, Jehan."

"Okay. Everyone's getting antsy."

"Alright, alright. We're coming."

Soon, the four ladies of Rosiary head downstairs with the second-in-command of the royal guard.

When Astrid begins opening her presents, she thanks each and every guest after each and every gift. The guests get a little restless after a while, but they know that this is a once-in-a-lifetime opportunity – Astrid's fifth birthday.

"Alright, it's time for us to get this little lady to bed. Say goodnight and goodbye, Astrid."

"Night and bye-bye." Astrid says, waving to her party guests.

"Good night, Lady Astrid." The guests reply.

Soon, Astrid is put to bed, and Kit, now well into his prime, kisses his daughter and daughter-in-law before they, too, head to bed after a long and enjoyable party.

That night, Asmi is carefully watching over their goddaughter when a figure knocks Asmi unconscious. When Asmi awakens, Astrid's bed is empty.

They sound the alarm, waking up everyone in the Morrison estate, not wanting anyone to be asleep while Astrid is out there, being kidnapped by Aileen-knows-who.

Calla and Katherine clutch each other as Asmi explains that Astrid has been taken.

"I don't know where she is or who took her, but I will stop at absolutely nothing to find her and bring her back home, alive and well." Asmi says as they mount a horse with the Morrison's royal guard, and they head out to try and find the missing five-year-old.

The night is long and dark, and Asmi and the Morrison's royal guard stop at nothing to try and find Lady Astrid, but, eventually, they become exhausted and stop their search to go to one of the lodges in Rosiary.

Astrid is found the next day, and, although she's a bit beaten, bloodied, and bruised, she's otherwise fine.

Her Auncle Asmi takes her in their arms and they all head back to the Morrison estate.

When they reach the estate, a loud boom is heard in the distance, and the royal guard, with Asmi and Astrid in tow, head into the estate to drop off Astrid and Asmi before investigating the sound.

They soon return, and they make a public announcement to the world: the world is coming to an end.

"Asmi told me years ago that the end of the world would come sooner than we think. But I didn't think it would be *this* soon." Calla says, holding a sleepy Astrid in her arms.

"Yes, but I wasn't predicting that the end of the world would be *today*!"

"I'm sure you weren't, Asmi. So what do we do?"

"We prepare for the beginning of the end."

"And how do we go about doing that?"

"We gather nonperishable foods, water, weapons, clothing, other things that will help us, should we need to evacuate."

"And where exactly would we evacuate to?"

"The Hartreusian castle. That place is impenetrable, and would be a good place for home base...that was an unintentional rhyme." Jehan says, chuckling a bit, despite the situation that's upon all of them. No one else laughs.

"Well, we'd better get going if we're going to make it there. How do you suggest we get there, Jehan?" Katherine asks.

"We take carriages and horses."

"Good man. Let's get going before something happens and we can't leave." Asmi says, taking a still-sleeping Astrid from Calla.

Once the Morrison estate – family and servants alike – has been evacuated and they all head to the Hartreusian castle.

They get there and enter the castle. Astrid, having been cooped up in the Morrison estate for most of her life, gets to looking around with her Auncle Asmi as they begin to explore the castle. Asmi shows Astrid the library, which is sizably bigger than the one they have in the Morrison estate.

After Asmi and Astrid spend some time in the Hartreusian royal library, they borrow some books for Asmi to read to their god-daughter.

When they both rejoin the group, Luana is talking with them.

"I suggest we talk to Hazel...I-I mean *Aileen*. She may know what to do."

"With the end of the world upon us, my transforming powers don't really work all that well. So, you're stuck with little old Hazel."

"And that's fine by us, Hazel. Come. Everyone, to the saferoom. We've expanded it to make it hold as many people in the entire royal family as possible." Nona says.

The group of royals, with Asmi and Hazel in tow, head to the saferoom, which is stocked with supplies and things for entertainment.

A year passes, and things are going pretty well in the saferoom. New friends are made, supplies are replenished, and things are learned.

There are footsteps coming from above the saferoom, and, soon, an explosion is heard and shaking is felt from inside the saferoom.

When the shaking stops and no explosions can be heard, Asmi heads up to check on the status of the Hartreusian castle.

When they come back, their face is hopeful.

"Well, the castle is still standing. But I'm sure it's going to get worse before it gets better."

Another year passes, and, every month, Asmi goes up in gear to make sure that the castle is still standing.

One day, however, years later, when they come back from a check, their face is solemn.

"The castle is in ruins. The entire town is, really."

| 23 |

The New World

As the royals leave their saferoom, they don't believe what they're seeing, and it takes a few minutes for them to register what they see in front of them: as far as their eyes can see, Hartreusia is in ruins, filled with smoke and burned to the ground.

When they try to contact their outside sources from the other countries of Gnypso, the picture and audio are both fuzzy, but they're able to make out the words "fire", "smoke", and "destruction".

"I can't believe it. Asmi was actually right."

"I was?"

"Yes. You told me, years ago, that the end of the world would be sooner than we'd think, and now look where we're standing: in the ruins of our planet Gnypso, with no hope of seeing anyone outside of our little group."

"So, what do we do?"

"We search for survivors. Hazel?"

"Yes, Calla?"

"We'll need you to use your powers to go back to the Broken Realm to see how everyone there is faring. You know everyone by name and face, do you not?"

"As Aileen, I would, but as Hazel, like I've told you a hundred times already, my knowledge and power are both limited."

"And you can't turn back into Aileen, Grandma Hazel?" Now-sixteen-year-old Astrid asks her great-great-grandmother.

"I can try. Stand back, everyone."

Everyone stands back and Hazel focuses her power into trying to transform back into Aileen. But being stuck as Hazel for so many years has put a block on her power, and, try as she might, she's not able to transform into Aileen.

"I'm sorry...I'm stuck as Hazel, which means I cannot go to the Broken Realm unless one of you sacrifices yourselves or me."

"Well, we're not going to do that, Hazel."

"Speak for yourself, Asmi! You thought you'd murdered me, and then Calla, poor, poor Calla was stuck having PTSD flashbacks for a very long time."

"But I'm fine now, Grandma Hazel."

"I know you are, child. But that doesn't make it any easier for any of us. We need to find a way to get to the Broken Realm, so I can make sure my other children and my subjects are all doing alright."

"If I could be of any assistance, dears."

Hazel screams, recognizing that voice. She turns, and sees her twin sister Willow, in spirit form.

"Willow! You old bean, what are you doing here?" Hazel runs over and hugs her twin sister.

"I'm here to help you all, Hazelnut."

"I'm so confused. How can Aileen have a twin sister, plus be Qhuvelia's sister at the same time? Who is Aileen's mother?!" Asmi asks, very puzzled.

"It's called having a second life, Asmi. When my mother, then the allmother herself, gave birth, she had both myself and Willow. Later, she had a third baby, Qhuvelia. But there was something different about Qhuvelia: something evil was afoot...and we couldn't figure out what it was. Until she got older, when she developed abilities that no one had ever seen. She had powers that neither Willow nor I could have or understand."

"Grandma Hazel, what was your mother's name?" Astrid asks.

"Her name was Amalthea. Anyway, where was I?"

"Qhuvelia having powers no one had ever seen?"

"Right, right. Thank you, Katie. Qhuvelia developed powers that involved dark magic, magic that is evil and that no human should ever deal with: possession, manipulation, and mind-control, being able to transport someone into the past."

"Transport someone into the past? You mean like the time Celeste transported herself and me into the past to the accident and to when Nona and I met?"

"Yes. And when you took those time trips, some of Celeste's dark magic *and* light magic began flowing through your veins."

"But I've never used dark magic. Doesn't that mean it would just drain right out of me?"

"No, Luana. Neither light and dark magic can drain out of you if you developed the gift of spell casting later in life, instead of when one was ten years old."

"I see. Are there more than two kinds of magic?"

"No. There are just those two kinds: dark and light. But it's up to the individual spell caster on how to use their magic, not anyone else. So, if they somehow come in possession of dark magic, they must be taught to use it wisely, and not for evil purposes like my sister Qhuvelia does."

"Is there any way we could stop Qhuvelia, even as mortals?"

"I'm afraid only one that has faced her or one of her minions before and won will be able to face her, and they must be a spell caster."

Everyone immediately looks at Calla Lilly.

"Oh, no! It can't be me. Yes, I fought her minions in my youth, but I can't fight her! I've got my two kids to think about."

"Your two kids that are almost fully grown? Mum, we'll be fine. Besides, Mama will still be here, won't you, Mama?"

"Of course, darling. But, Calla, I don't feel comfortable sending you out alone to face Qhuvelia, especially when you don't have the best magic training."

"What about that time I fought against Kazamir? I could just use Lightning Basalt on Qhuvelia, and dodge whatever attacks she throws at me, and I'll win. Simple as that."

"But it's not that simple, child. Kazamir may be more experienced than Qhuvelia in the field, but Qhuvelia has more magic experience in combat, and not just because of her age. You see, she and Willow and I used to engage in fights, and when Qhuvelia was first born, she was a very feisty infant. There was nothing anyone, not even our mother or father, could do to calm her when she was having a screaming fit."

"Why would she have screaming fits?"

"Because she was a baby, little Celeste. And she was a stubborn baby at that, refusing to do anything that she couldn't do on her own. She held her head up just a few hours after she was born! Held her own bottle at two months old. Need I go on?"

"We get it, Grandma Hazel. Qhuvelia was a special child. A stubborn child, but a special child nonetheless." Astrid tells her great-great-grandmother.

"Don't I know it! Qhuvelia was special, stubborn and a snothead. But, most importantly, she was the baby of the family, and Willow and I had to look out for her."

"I get that. I had to look out for my younger sisters all the time as kids, and I still look out for Victoria and Celeste to this day."

"Yeah, more than we'd like, to be honest, sis." Celeste tells her oldest sister.

There's suddenly a boom coming from the distance, and the group goes to investigate it, and they find Qhuvelia and her undead army rising up to fight the mortals.

"We need to do something to help the mortals. But what?" Luana asks.

"Stand together, band together and fight together! It's what we do best, Luana!" Hazel exclaims.

What's left of the Hartreusian royal guard approaches the royals, led by Matilde, Emmitt's sister.

"We came as soon as we saw you in the distance. We're here to assist you in any way that we can."

"I don't know how you could assist us, Matilde. Calla is the one who needs to go and fight Qhuvelia and her undead army." Emmitt says, looking in the direction of his sister's voice.

"So, what do we do? Just send her out without backup?" Katie asks.

"That's all you *can* do, Katie. I need to face Qhuvelia alone. And who knows? Maybe she's gotten weaker over the years."

"That's where you're wrong, Calla. Hazel and I both know that Qhuvelia has only gotten stronger over the years." Asmi tells their niece.

"So...do I have any chance of beating her by myself?"

"There is a slight possibility that you *will* be able to beat her alone. But there's also the chance that she could kill you outright, and we'd be left without our most important asset."

"So...I really *am* the chosen one?"

"Yes. And we believe in you, Calla Lilly Morrison. Only *you* can put a stop to this war. Only *you* can figure out how to beat Qhuvelia." Asmi says, placing their hands on Calla's shoulders.

"Without any outside help?"

"We're afraid so, Calla. But we believe in you, kiddo. Your journey, your *arrival* has been foretold since the old world ended and the new world began." Kit tells his stepdaughter.

"Alright. I'll go."

"Don't go getting a big head there, Calla. You're still a novice at magic, even if you have been training under me since you first got your powers."

"I understand, Grandma Hazel."

"Good. We'll all be waiting right here for you to return. And thank you for saving us all."

"Don't thank me yet. I haven't exactly done anything to beat her."

"While that may be true, you still have more power flowing through those veins of yours than you realize."

"I understand. Well, here I go."

"You've got this, my sister." Celeste says, hugging her oldest sister.

"Thank you, Celeste."

"Hey, and if you don't make it, say 'hello' to your mum for us, will you?" Victoria asks, tears welling in her eyes.

"I'll do just that, Vic. Though I don't expect to be gone very long. Just hope for the best, and prepare for the worst."

With many hugs to and from her family members, Calla walks away from her family behind her, and to her enemy in front of her.

It takes a long while for Calla to reach Qhuvelia's base camp, but, when she finally does, she takes in the broken world that she's supposedly going to save all on her own.

From her hiding place, Calla sees Kazamir talking strategy with Qhuvelia.

"Ah, Miss Calla Lilly. How nice of you to join us!" Mya, Kazamir's second-in-command, says, approaching Calla from behind.

"Mya? What is it? Who's there?"

"I found this girl hiding and spying on you and Her Wickedness, Kazamir."

"Bring her to me, Mya."

"Right away, Qhuvelia. Let's go, you."

| 24 |

The Battle For the Ages

Mya brings Calla to Qhuvelia, shoving her to the ground and pressing her face into the mud.

"Bow before our goddess, our true queen, mortal."

"You're a mortal, just like me."

"Yes, but at least *I* have a home to go back to. You don't."

"At least *I* have a family to return to, instead of bosses and minions."

"The bosses and minions *are* my family, Morrison. We have a bond like no other."

"Serving someone that only serves herself, and not others?"

"How dare you speak so ill of our queen! She is more of a goddess than you'll ever be, more of a royal than anyone you know will ever be."

"And what do you suggest that I do? Run back to my family with my tail between my legs? Just keel over? Fight the most wicked of the wicked?"

"There's only one thing you *can* do here, Calla. Submit yourself to Qhuvelia, and all will be right in the world."

"Never! I would never join someone like Qhuvelia. But what I *will* do is fight her. To the death."

"Mya, bring her forward. I have an interest in making her my prisoner."

"Move it, Calla. And don't you make me tell you again to bow before Her Wickedness."

Calla is forced to kneel before Qhuvelia, who takes her face in her grasp.

"It's sad, really. Someone as simple as you, a mortal, was sent to try and defeat *me*? I am more powerful than you know."

"You're a stubborn goddess, I'll give you that."

"As are you. Because you are the great-granddaughter of my sister, Aileen, you, too, are a goddess. And us goddesses need to stick together, to create a new world, a *better* world."

"What?"

"Did Hazel not tell you? Pfft, figures. So typical of my sister to not tell our most important asset of her true identity."

"Why did you say 'our'? I belong only to Aileen, and not to you."

"How soon you forget. That Auncle Asmi of yours forced you to give up your soul to me. I can't believe you've forgotten such an important fact about yourself. Then again, you were so young when your soul was given to me."

"And what does that have to do with anything? I'll never join you, Qhuvelia."

"How naïve. There's nothing more pathetic than someone with a savior-complex. You *will* join me, Calla. Ha. As if you had any other choice."

Calla steps forward to fight Qhuvelia one-on-one.

"Oh, you want a battle, do you? Well, give it your best shot, mortal. I'll make sure you never see the light of day ever again."

"Bring it on, old lady."

"Old lady? I take that as a compliment, dear. I am far older than anyone realizes. Of course, I do lack in the wisdom both of my sisters have."

"Are we going to just banter, or are we going to fight?"

"Very well. If it's a fight that you want, then it's a fight you shall have. Kazamir, be my second. Mya, be Calla's second."

"Why do I have to be the mortal's second?"

"Are you questioning my authority, Mya?"

"N-no, Your Wickedness."

"That's what I thought."

Mya and Calla go to one of the corners of the clearing where they stand.

Mya walks up to Kazamir.

"Tell Qhuvelia to give the mortal hell."

"Aren't you supposed to be on the mortal's side?"

"Only because Qhuvelia told me to be. But I still want Qhuvelia to be the one that wins, so she can take over the world. Are you still not her second-in-command?"

"No, I am not. And why should I be? We all know that Asmi is more powerful than I."

"While that may be true, you have more experience than them, you could easily take them down without hesitation."

"Yes, but –"

"But what?"

"They're my *child*."

"So?"

"What do you mean 'so'? I've lost Celeste and her twin brother Quentin, along with the son that took my place at the gallows. I have countless other more children, and who knows how many of them have survived the uprising of Qhuvelia and her undead army?"

"We may never know, because you've slept with and impregnated countless people. So many that you could never know how many children you have."

"Are we going to help Qhuvelia beat this mortal or not?"

"We are."

"Let's get on with it, then. Go to your corner, and get ready to cheer on the mortal."

"As if I'd ever cheer on anyone other than – "

"Enough banter, you two, and let's get this battle started!"

"Yes, Qhuvelia."

As Mya walks back to Calla, she sticks her tongue out at Kazamir. He returns the gesture.

Qhuvelia gets ready to beat Calla to a pulp, using only magic.

"You've got this, Qhuvelia. This will be so easy for you."

"I hope not, Kazamir."

"Oh?"

"I love a challenge. Surely you'd remember that."

"My name isn't Shirley."

"That's not what I meant, Kazamir. I can't believe you're making jokes at a time like this."

"Oh, this will be an easy battle for you, Your Wickedness. I can guarantee that."

"Don't make any promises or guarantees you cannot keep, Kazamir. It will only hinder your progress in becoming my new second-in-command."

"Your new second-in-command? *Me?*"

"Yes. You have great potential. It's just that Asmi started working for me long before you did. You were too busy playing around."

"No more of that, Qhuvelia, I can – "

"Don't say that you can guarantee not playing around, Kazamir. It's in your nature."

"Are you going to fight the mortal or are we just going to exchange words back and forth?"

"Let's get on with it."

Qhuvelia takes the paces towards Calla, and Calla does the same towards Qhuvelia.

"Are you ready for this, mortal?"

"I don't know. Are you ready for this, you old crone?"

"I am. Magic at the ready. Oh, and no Lightning Basalt. I heard that's how you beat Kazamir your first time using magic."

"Fair enough."

"Ten paces, then we give each other our best spells. Whoever gets beaten down first for at least five seconds, the other person wins."

"And you're using the term 'person' lightly, are you not?"

"Clever girl. Ten paces, back to back."

The two goddesses turn back to back and take ten steps away from each other. They then face each other, and Calla whispers "Purity of Strength".

When Qhuvelia casts the magic containing the elements at Calla, it knocks Calla back a little, but she's still standing.

"Ah, using 'Purity of Strength', are we? Well, two can play at that game. Abracadabra."

"Hey, I didn't use the impervious spell, just the spell to make me stronger than usual! That's not fair!"

"Life isn't fair, Calla Lilly. The sooner you realize that, the sooner you can change your perspective."

"Let's just get this over with."

"Done."

Qhuvelia and Calla cast different magic spells at each other, and they are both knocked to the ground at different times. But they get right back up and continue fighting.

It goes on for hours, and neither of them are yielding to the other.

"Come on, Calla Lilly Morrison. Surely you know you cannot defeat me alone."

"I may not be alone, then. Shall we ask our seconds to fight alongside us?"

"Very well. Mya, Kazamir! To your places. There is a score we need to settle."

"Yes, Qhuvelia." Kazamir and Mya both groan out.

Mya stands next to Calla while Kazamir stands next to Qhuvelia.

"Wait...how is this going to work since I don't have any magic?"

"I'll supply you with some of my power."

The battle resumes and there is nothing Calla or Mya can do to defeat Qhuvelia and Kazamir, even together.

Back at the base of where Calla's family is, the group is fighting people off, trying to spare the children that are among them any pain.

"We need to get to Calla, Luana! She may need us!" Nona tells her wife.

"And leave the rest of our family defenseless? I think not, Nona!"

"I understand that, Luana, but one of us has to go and help Calla fight Qhuvelia."

"Only Calla can defeat Qhuvelia. No one is allowed to assist her. Those are the rules of the magic duel." Hazel says.

"While that may be true, she still needs someone to cheer her on. Is cheering her on against the rules?" Nona asks.

"No. I'll go and cheer her on. You all stay here. I'll be back before you know it, peoples!" Hazel exclaims.

Hazel runs as fast as her little legs can carry her to the duel spot.

Calla and Qhuvelia are in the thick of battle, Calla getting weaker by the moment, and Qhuvelia not as well off, either.

"Grandma Hazel? What are you doing here? You can't be here! It's too dangerous!"

"Dangerous, shmangerous! I'll be just fine, Calla! You're forgetting I'm a goddess! As are you! Use your goddess-y powers to fight Qhuvelia!"

"I can't, Grandma Hazel! I don't know how!"

"Just focus your power and focus on beating Qhuvelia to a literal pulp! She may be my sister, but she's wicked! She needs to be told what her place is in the world!"

"I understand, Grandma Hazel. But what if I'm not strong enough to beat her?"

"You must beat her, or we're all doomed, Calla! You must try as hard as you can!"

"I'll try, Grandma Hazel! That's the best I can do!"

"I don't doubt your abilities, Miss Calla Lilly! Now kick her butt!"

Calla walks up to Qhuvelia and kicks her in the butt, surprising her.

"I didn't mean that literally, Calla! Oh, well."

"Did you just...kick my butt, mortal?"

"Your sister told me to!"

"Oh, well, if it's a physical fight that you want, and not a magical one, it's a fight I'm willing to have with you. Hand-to-hand combat only. No kicking unless absolutely necessary. The same rules apply – whoever gets beaten down for about five seconds, the other person wins!"

"Very well. Let's get this over with."

"And here I thought we were having fun! Begin, and give it your best shot, Calla. I will miss our talks."

"What talks? We haven't talked to each other at all, except for witty banter!"

"And that's the best kind of talk to have!"

"Not heart-to-heart?"

"Don't go getting sentimental on me, Calla. Are we fighting or are we just talking about fighting?"

"Let's fight."

Punches are thrown towards one another, and Calla and Qhuvelia both get beat up by each other.

Soon, Calla is beaten and she is knocked down by Qhuvelia, nearly unconscious.

"Had enough, Calla?"

"Never." Calla says, spitting up blood and one of her teeth.

"Very well. Magic only from now on. Punches don't have the same volume as magic does."

Calla gets up and begins fighting with magic against Qhuvelia. The two goddesses fight each other, and, soon, Calla is knocked unconscious.

"Get up, Calla! You need to get up!" Hazel calls out.

"No outside help! Especially not from you, Hazel!"

"Too bad, Qhuvelia! You can't stop me!"

"Mya, Kazamir! Tie the old crone up!"

"Right away, Qhuvelia."

Mya and Kazamir head over to Hazel and tie her up as Calla is still unconscious.

"Please, child. You must get up. You mustn't give up."

"I'm afraid – I'm afraid it's too late for me, Hazel. Tell my family...I love them."

Calla succumbs to a bright light.

When she wakes up, it looks like she's in the Broken Realm.

The Broken Realm is filled with columns, clouds and castles. It is splendorous.

A woman surrounded by light approaches Calla.

"Calla, my daughter. Welcome to the Broken Realm."

"Mum?!"

| 25 |

The End and the Beginning

"It is I, your mother, Celeste Riker, Calla. I've been watching over you for so many years."

"And...I'm – I'm dead, aren't I?"

"Yes, you are."

"Qhuvelia beat me. I lost. Wait...doesn't my soul still belong to Qhuvelia?"

"It did. Until you sacrificed yourself for the greater good. Hazel – Aileen – let you pass into our true home – the home of the broken, far beyond Gnypso – the Broken Realm."

"So, this is really the Broken Realm?"

"Yes. Now, come here. I haven't hugged you in decades."

Calla walks over to her mother and the two hug for the first time since Calla was a toddler.

"Let me look at you."

Calla lets Celeste look at her thoroughly.

"Mum?"

"Hmm?"

"Is there any way I could go back to the land of the living?"

"Unless Qhuvelia is somehow beaten, I'm afraid you'll be here for the rest of eternity."

"So, forever, then?"

"I'm afraid so, Calla. But Hazel will have to tell everyone that you're gone."

"Poor Hazel. She and I got along so well, even before her death."

"I know you did, sweetheart. Come. Let me show you around the Broken Realm."

"Mum, can I ask you something?"

"Of course, Calla."

"What happened to my baby sibling?"

"She's here, Calla. I named her Heather."

"Heather. A beautiful name."

"Thank you, Calla. I'll take you to all of your relatives that were lost during the Indigonian manor explosion."

"Okay." Hand-in-hand, mother and daughter walk around the Broken Realm, Celeste telling her daughter all about what is in the Broken Realm: there are shops and places to eat, places for rest, places for leisure and games, places to see, people to meet and things to do.

"It's beautiful here, Mum."

"I thought you might like it."

"Mum?"

"Yes?"

"Is it true that I'm a goddess?"

"Yes, it is. You inherited the title from Hazel...well, Aileen, as she's known here."

"And her daughter Era is really in charge now?"

"Yes. It hasn't been easy having Era as our ruler, but we've grown to love having her here in place of Aileen."

"And what about the other gods and goddesses of Destiny? Loana, Nellie, Erik, Irah, and Sena? What do they do here?"

"Why, they control their specific powers based on their given name and role in life. Era stopped giving and slowing and stopping time, so the end of the world came. The rest of the gods and goddesses are a bit weaker than they were before Aileen left."

"So, Qhuvelia stole their magic?"

"How did you ever come to know that?"

"Lucky guess, Mum."

"You're smart, Calla. You take after your father in that regard."

"So...what am I going to do?"

"I don't know, Calla. I simply don't know. I am not a goddess myself, despite Hazel being my grandmother."

"So, it skipped your generation?"

"Actually, being a god or goddess skipped *two* generations, since Kazamir is not a god either. What you have, Calla, is more special than anything you've ever known. But being a goddess doesn't mean sitting on a throne and telling the ones below you what to do."

"What does it mean, then? Being there for people and making small sacrifices for them?"

"Exactly, my Calla."

"Mum?"

"Yes, Calla?"

"Will I ever get to go back to my family? I'm sure they miss me."

"That's the second time you've asked something like that, Calla, and the answer is still the same. There's no way for you to go back to the living world unless Qhuvelia is beaten."

"Oh. Sorry for asking twice, Mum."

"It's alright. You seem like you want to go back to the living world. Is there something wrong with the Broken Realm?"

"Oh, no, Mum, it's beautiful. It just...doesn't feel like home to me. I'm sure I'll get used to it soon enough."

"You haven't even been here two hours, and you're already feeling homesick. That's surprising. You always adapted to change very well when you were younger. Like when Victoria was born, you got along with her very well."

"I know I did, Mum. But my sister is different than a new world. Yes, she's a world of her own, but that doesn't mean I'm an inhabitant of it."

"I get what you mean, Calla."

Calla and Celeste stop at a viewpoint, where they can look at the current state of Gnypso.

It's in ruins, and Qhuvelia and her undead army is taking prisoners, killing some and enslaving others.

"It's awful down there."

"Well, what are you doing just standing there, Calla? Come back with me to Gnypso!"

Celeste and Calla turn to see Hazel in all her glory, ready to welcome Calla back to Gnypso.

"Hazel, you know what Great-Grandma Amalthea would say. Once a goddess comes here, there's no choice to go back to Gnypso...it simply isn't done."

"And where is my mother now?"

"Well, she's – "

"She's enjoying her retirement, that's where she is."

"HAZEL!"

"Uh-oh."

Calla, Celeste and Hazel turn to the voice, and a figure with a glow greater than anything Hazel has ever emitted, appears out of the clouds.

"Mother! How have you been?"

"How have I been? There's a war going down on Gnypso, and you're asking how I've been? I'm surprised at you, Hazel."

"You are?"

"Yes! Your sister needs to be stopped from creating even more destruction than she already has."

"And, Mum, how do you suppose we do that?"

"By sending the chosen one back to Gnypso."

"Calla? Absolutely not! She's sacrificed herself once already, do we really need to sacrifice her again?"

"She won't be sacrificed again, Hazel. She'll have an army consisting of the rest of the gods and goddesses. Looks like I'm coming out of retirement early."

"Mum, that won't be necessary."

"With all due respect, Your Majesty, I don't need any help."

"Oh, but you do, Calla."

"I do?"

"Yes. There's no one that can beat my youngest alone. Everyone needs help sometimes, even a goddess."

"So...I'm not going back to Gnypso alone?"

"No. You'll have an army of your relatives, mortal and god and goddess alike, to help you fight Qhuvelia."

"I see. Thank you, Amalthea."

"You're welcome. Now go. Go kick Qhuvelia's butt."

"And how do you suppose we do that?"

"By working together, Calla. That's the only way you *can* do that!"

"Yes, ma'am!"

With an army behind her, Calla leads her family members and fellow gods and goddesses back down to Gnypso.

"QHUVELIA!" Calla screams.

Qhuvelia looks back in fear and sees the very opponent she had thought she's beaten.

"Ah, Miss Calla Lilly. How nice to see you again. I thought we'd lost you."

"You did lose me, but I'm back and better than ever. CHARGE!"

Calla's army charges towards Qhuvelia and her army, and the fight is grand, grander than any fight that any of them have ever fought before.

In the end, with swords, axes, hatchets, and shields clashing, Calla and her army are victorious, sending Qhuvelia and her army back to the underworld.

Once the battle is over, the Gnypsonians join together to rebuild their beloved planet.

It takes months to rebuild the castles, manors, estates, homes, and businesses from scratch, and there are many hardships along the way, but they manage to finish it by the start of the next year.

A grand feast is held just days after the Feast of the Goddess, and everyone on Gnypso, from the past and present, gods and humans alike, are in attendance.

Calla looks back on her work, as the new goddess of love, and she smiles. As she plays games with her children and grandchildren, she knows that her time on Gnypso is limited, but her time in the Broken Realm is anything but limited. Aileen/Hazel takes her place back in the Broken Realm as the ruler, and her mother Amalthea goes back into retirement.

Calla is reunited with her mother, being able to come and go from the Broken Realm as she pleases, knowing that her duties there need to be fulfilled, but she isn't in any rush, since she has all the time on Gnypso that she wants.

Kit and Inge eventually get married, and they rule as co-lord and co-lady of Rosiary, alongside Emmitt and Isabella. The four rule together, live together and laugh together. The relationships Calla has formed grow stronger over her remaining years on Gnypso. She reaches the Broken Realm long after her wife, children and grandchildren do, and her Auncle Asmi – who is as faithful to Aileen as ever – is there to greet her.

All in all, Calla's life had its ups and downs, but being a goddess has its ups and downs as well.

No matter what Calla has gone through, she's always known that she would never go through anything alone.